Comes Voyager at Last

A Tale of Return to Africa

KOFI N. AWOONOR

Africa World Press, Inc.
P.O. Box 1892
Trenton, New Jersey 08607

Africa World Press, Inc.

P.O. Box 1892
Trenton, New Jersey 08607

First Printing 1992

All characters in this tale exist only in the land of stories and bear no resemblance to real persons living or dead. Anyone who says he recognizes himself in this tale is an extravagantly imaginative liar, and has no truth in him.

Book design and typesetting by Malcolm Litchfield
This book is composed in Stone Informal

Cover Illustration by Carles J. Juzang

Library of Congress Catalog Card Number: 91-75602

ISBN: 0-86543-262-7 Cloth
0-86543-263-5 Paper

The voice I heard this passing night was heard
In ancient days by emperor and clown:
Perhaps the self-same song that found a path
Through the sad heart of Ruth, when sick for home
She stood in tears amid the alien corn.

Keats: "Ode to a Nightingale"

Now the labourer's task is done,
Now the battle day is over,
Now upon the farther shore
Lands the voyager at last

Methodist Hymn

To

Haki Madhubuti, Jean Small, Martin Carter, Eddie Brathwaite, Quincy Troupe, Harvey Naarendorp, Chas Mynals, Abdias Nascimento and all the extended family members in Babylon

and to

the memory of my brother and comrade Neville Augustus Dawes who revealed to me the miracle of story time, and gave us hope for liberation.

THE DESERT, MAN'S DEATH LAND, birthplace. Washed over rolling sand dunes. Time stood still in these grains of sand. The toothy grin of the acacia, gnarled by centuries of heat. The desert was not long. Our journey commenced at its edge, a dreary outpost which could have been the terminus. Then the chains were fastened upon us, accompanied by the barking of dogs and men, the crying of children and the whimpering of women. Order came that our march southwards should begin at dawn. It is not easy to recreate the memory of that journey. But that memory hangs on like the tangible thread in a historic fabric long worn.

The days were hot and sultry. The sun hung in our firmament, indolent and mute. Only the breathing pores of our glistening skins howled at intervals of fatigue and sorrow. We plodded on, our weary feet dragging through sandy fields, skirting what could have been human habitations on our silent march. There must have been about a hundred of us, men, women, and infants hardly weaned, babies on their mothers' back. The little ones died one a day. Not that there could have been any help for them. The laws of our fate had sealed all avenues of human help. We had been condemned to the bitter sorrows of hell.

At noon on the third day, weary of feet and almost unaware of pain becuase of the numbness in our hearts, our march wound up near a little hamlet. The desert sun had been long setting sorrowing. The village smoke from the few bustling homesteads curled into the face of the yellow sun. On the village outskirts, the yearly grass hedgegrown green sustained by the cold night and its dew, and the few misty tear drops of a sad and unwilling heaven. In lonely tufts of grass, shades for dwarfmen and the first terrible violence of colour for days in this wide expanse attracted our attention. We had stopped near a verdant plot, our captors and owners debating whether we should enter into this village. Our supplies were running out. The little that was left of the brackish water was shared among us. We drank mouthfuls. In the eyes of some, this libation was a wasted act, for death had moved into their shadows and would take them away before a new sun rose. We had wandered, as if without direction, guided by the stars, the processional terminals of long and weary days of tears and sorrow. And this desert, once ploughed by our feet, fashioned the eternal frenzy and the howling waves of our history. The sun, whose children we were, took not away from our hearts the warmth and the binding power of his secret covenant. Could we too not claim the rights and the expectation of a chosen people? Towards our heavens, and alongside the agonized wail of solitary birds over the wild sand track, some of us raised prayers for deliverance in infinite silence.

It was that hour before men and creatures retire. Our entrance was unannounced. There was a huge baobab in the centre of the village. It looked like the home of a god. There we were led in a caravan of sorrow. We were made to crouch on the ground while our captors went into the western end of the village to bargain for food. Silence, which had become our regular companion, had not deserted us. She kept with us even now a more ominous comradeship than in all our days. There was near me an old man grey and weak of body, a wheezing sound emanating from his congested chest. He kept on repeating something in a strange language of perhaps one of the northern riverain people. His eyes were as yellow as the setting sun. His grey had been induced by the recent sorrow of our capitivity.

After a time, I noticed that what he was repeating was the name of someone, a man , woman, child or god close to him. The

word had assumed for him a talismanic power and quality upon which he hung some vague and intangible expectation. What was he hoping for from the word? Whenever our eyes came near to meeting, I was aware of an impenetrable visionary look that pierced our present sorrow beyond time. He remained in his crouching position; it was a posture of prayer; yet there was nothing distinctly spiritual about him except his hollow eyes and his vision. Perhaps already some internal resignation had taken over, and his words and looks were only the visible manifestations of the ultimate outrage of death that would be wrought. He was the lamb of the sacrifice. Unaware of the pain of the rope and the suffering of the beatings, he kept his bleating on through the village lane behind the priest on his way to the shrine where his throat will be cut.

We huddled together in the hollow arms of the baobab for hours. The old man kept up the word, now growing in volume and passionate intensity, acquiring by each utterance the frenzy of a command and the desperate expectations of an incantation. Did he hope that whoever he was calling would hear him? And if he heard, what was he to do? Around us were the mothers now suckling their babies amidst a low moaning sound as of doom. Some were asleep, giving off gentle snores, their hands folded as pillows beneath their heads as much as the chains would allow.

Long after darkness descended, those of our captors who had left earlier returned, followed by long gowned messengers carrying basins of food and pots and gourds of water. Our evening meal was a silent hurried affair, consisting of a strange type of cornmeal or bread, bean cakes and water. Many could not even swallow the first morsels they put in their mouths. Mercifully, our captors had agreed that we would spend the night in this village and proceed upon the first light of dawn on our southward march.

There was a fitful silence which enveloped us as we slept, continuing our frightful nightmares, darkly locked in the prison of our fears. That night, it must have been before the cold winds of midnight, the old man died. He had kept on his magical word till sleep took it away from him. But even in his sleep, we could hear him pronouncing the sibilants of this mystic word which I cannot now recall. Soon he opened his eyes with a start and proceeded to adjust his arms an legs in a long stretch in which I could hear his muscles cracking loud and clear. He was a small wiry man, light-skinned, with a huge forehead in which rolled two large red eyes. On his left cheek a wound was faintly healing. His chest was narrow. It emitted an independent squeak that became outrageous whenever he was agitated. He started as if from a secret dream, and after cracking his muscles in that involuntary stretch, he turned towards me staring fearsomely into my eyes. There was something he wanted to say. And he wanted to say it badly, but he knew I did not understand his language. For, on the very first day when we had arrived at the departure town, he spoke to me in a language full of sibilants and hisses. I shook my head signaling that I did not understand. But now, there was speech bursting out of his narrow heart to be delivered. There was no longer the awareness that I spoke not his tongue. Suddenly he clutched my arms with his tiny hands, dry and strung with veins woven into the knotted maze of his palms. In his eyes was the most horrible look I have ever seen in man or beast, a deep cavernous gaze burning with a million fires. The eternal hope that kept perpetual vigilance in his large rolling eyes had fled. And in its place was revealed the naked horror of death. In a hushed conspiratorial voice he whispered to me once more the word he had spoken throughout the journey. And then he let go of my hand. His eyes rolled as he rolled back upon the grey earth of this oasis. And in a moment he was dead.

Sleep went on for the others as if nothing had happened. They were not even aware of a death in our midst. Some of the children were still crying. The old man lay on the spot where he fell when the first lights of dawn caught him. He was serene and almost flesh filled now in death. When our captors discovered he had died, they ordered three of us to dig a hole and bury him. We buried him in a quick and shallow hole because the order had come for us to strike camp and move on.

IN ABOUT HALF AN HOUR my plane will take off. I will be flying back to the States. I have been here almost a year now.

Many people back in the States had warned me about Africa. I can recall the voices, hammering their points, poking me in the chest, cock-eyed, sober, drolling drunk, offering voluble admonition about Africa. There was old Doc at Jeff's Bar on 118 and Lenox, large like his Louisiana fields slowly but knowingly dying of some horrible hidden disease. Only he wasn't a doctor. He served as a medical orderly in some forgotten army unit during the second world war. You could see death, now an intimate companion, in his eyes, and life beaming in his drinking hours and beating hopefully in his left eye, the eye he squints as he takes a pull on his scotch and water. Yeah man, I been all over Africa, he would be saying, a sad distant look in his eyes. During the war that was. He was at Takoradi in the Gold Coast and in Cape Town. Yeah ... That was at Takoradi in the Gold Coast and in Cape Town. Yeah ... That was when the marines was marines, and no one cared a damn wheder your was colored or yella. Son, we me and a group of boys, was the deck hands, loadin and unloading. I suppose we was to work with the doc when the bombs fell; no bombs ever fell where we was. Lard, bull biscuits, salted pork, beer. Yeah, it was a good life. I figure that was when I put on this here weight. A lotta the lads just come out of the farms down south, some as green as a spinach patch, and didn't know what was going on. But they worked hard, I tell you, those niggers in them days sure work hard. No loafin and jivin around like today. Now and then the natives use ta wandor up the port and those guys don't look no different than the felahs from the dirt tracts and the farms back in Louisiana.

He will go and on, his voice a somnolent drone, deep and rich. He spoke pure poetry. And there was God's Chile Anderson, a native Alabamian who spent his youth in depression Chicago. I guess he was a delivery boy for one of the lower members of some thieving gang. Of course, every word God's Chile said was a lie, and old Doc, if he was around would correct his dates and places of some forgotten events. There wasn't much good feeling between the two of them. And God's Chile could raise a laugh. The night I came in bright-eyed and singing about going home to Africa and being with my people and touching the motherland, he stared at me for a long haul, a melancholy look steadily creeping into his mean eyes. After a lull of eternity, he mumbled to himself, yo ain't coming back kid if you go. All the boys were holding onto their glasses now, and even Sam White who ran a corner home cooking place that served the greasiest chicken in Harlem and who never rasied his head in his wine time lifted up his head and asked the question that I asked God's Chile. Why? After what seemed like a day he spoke in a soft low whisper bearing a hushed secret finality of pain and sorrow that was like the accompanying seriousness of the last judgement in front of God's throne and said: "You ain't coming back cause you's goin be eaten, thas why!"

A year in Africa. And tonight I am going back to America. There is no feeling like the home going feeling that I hear grips people who stray away from their homelands. It doesn't feel like I am going home. Just like returning to a place you used to know very well. Or not very well either. But a place you carry in your memory, a place built into an edifice of joy and sorrow, stamped at the end of the processional march of your folks in long gone days, where you learnt the syllables and movements of every sidewalk and mean alley, of every neighborhood drunk, every cop, trader and publican, every communal joy and sorrow. Alongside you carry your own private agony wrapped in a black cloth hidden underneath a public sorrow. A place where you walked in your own footsteps hearing the footfalls of folks before you, where you ate and drank meagre fares and bitter waters because you had no other choice. And it is only death that will snatch these away from you. Sometimes you walked in beautiful summer suns and cold winter evenings past derelict buildings, spent old men and weary youth nodding on street corners. And you carried the smell of your own violent blood and death in your wide nostrils.

In Africa on many occasions, guys will come over and seriously want to know what it is like in America. And I will repeat for them the impotent myths of my land of sojourn, the legends of Negrohood, of my flamboyant ancestors who worked the land, tall African giants of unremembered savannas not unaware of pain or degradation, men whose only claim to humanity seemed to have been as the poet said their signal endurance record under the whip, of men who sought refuge in the good book, and actually believed that they too, as God's children, will be given brightly colored robes to cover their nakedness on that glorious judgement day.

But let me quit this kind of talk and poetry and tell you how, when, what. It is what this tale is about.

My name is Marcus Garvey MacAndrews and that is my slave name. My African name is Sheik Lumumba Mandela. My ancestors must have been one of the first batch of Africans to arrive in the New World. And my father used to say this entitled us to more from the land than any refugee from Hungary and Latvia who came the other day. But that is

who deserves what?

politics. He always swore his great grand-uncle was lynched in Georgia for stealing an infant hog. Another family myth says he died for shooting at a white butcher. And I don't eat hog anymore having accepted the teachings of Elijah Mohammed the Messenger of Allah the Merciful.

But my folks didn't come from Georgia. My great grandmother and her brood of four sons and six girls received freedom and emancipation, and headed eastwards until they came to Charlottesville, Virginia, camp followers of Marse Lincum's boys. They settled here to work as handy men—reconstruction taught us skills—and farm hands for long standing white families. This period of my family's history, you will forgive me, is shrouded in mystery. For example, there was never much mention of the male side of the genealogical tree. And it seems our grand-uncle, the Georgian hog thief, was a pure invention of my imaginative father. But be that as it may, my family's genesis goes back to the civil war, a drift to Virginia, and a fantastic attachment to independence. After all, was not Virginia the home of Nat Turner who carried war and revolution to the oppressors in 1831? Didn't John Brown, a white man, storm Harper's Ferry and beckoned us to our historical march for freedom? Yes Sir! He sure did, that singular loving and selfless whiteman did signal our liberation!

My family, as I said, prospered during reconstruction. Those were the days of Governor Walker, and the Freedmen's Bureau, and Lumpkins slave jail; what was later turned into a school for niggers wasn't there when my folks arrived. This, as the story lingered, was called the Devil's Half Acre. And two of my uncles fought in the civil war, one serving on the USS Minnesota of whom General Butler once said: "No gun in the fleet was more steadily served than theirs and no men more composed than they when danger was supposed to be imminent." Supposed? The good general must be kidding, for there are stories in my family of how this grand-uncle's behinds were shot off a few days before the war was over. His name wasn't commmemorated on even a wooden plaque. And the other was among the one thousand Negro soldiers that died at the Battle of the Crater, July 30, 1864 when they marched in valiantly against superior fire after three white divisions had refused to advance.

My ancestors must have danced beneath the Emancipation Oak. They must have witnessed too the bringing home for burial the body of old John Holmes who was running for state senate in 1892.

And God was on our side too. The Mount Zion Baptist Church was our ancestral home, where over the mangled bodies of our dead, we screamed:

Free at last!
Free at last!
Thank God Almighty we are free at last!

But soon we scattered. The house-hold must have moved from Charlottesville to Norfolk, and a couple of relatives slipped down to North Carolina. But the hard core remained, its fortunes fluctuating. There were great years of prosperity, during the early days of Reconstruction when my grandfather, the last son, joined the railroads. He was too young to fight in the war. He rose to the enviable position of an assistant deputy cook on a pullman car on the Washingon-Chicago run. There was a picture of him hanging in the living room when I was a boy. He was a tall impressive figure in a grey trenchcoat fondly handling a frying pan, his insignia of office, amidst his comrades, some in aprons, guard caps and well-trimmed moustaches ante-bellum style. My father, who I suspect was jealous of his old man, used to say very litte of him. The two didn't get on apparently on account of my father putting Mary Ann the daughter of Mr. Morrison, the preacher of the Mount Zion Baptist Church, in the family way. And that was my mother, my elder brother Kelvin being the source of the eternal discord between my parents. My parents got married, however. Not doing so was unthinkable in those days. But my old man never forgave my mother for her carelessness and for setting for him what became famously known as The Trap.

From the picture of my grandfather, his impressive height, handsome face, high forehead and almost European features—a long herculean nose, clear grey eyes (no one ever told us from which side this Caucasian salvation came)—it would be concluded that my father would be a man of eminent proportions and distinguished features. It seemed fate arrested his growth and the God of my Baptist grandfather blighted and stunted him for life. My father was a dark little man with eyes like a rabbit's, neat feminine hands and the demeanour and gait of someone born not to toil in other people's vineyards, be it even the Lord's. He was born to be his own master. He had the manners of a gentleman, princely precious manners. He was always well dressed even in a threadbare suit of clothes. He possessed a deep bass voice which would have suited a singer. He was an aristocrat in his bearing. He hated sloppiness with a passion and punished it in his children with a venomous swiftness that defied the logic of his acute indigence and respectable mediocrity.

By the time I came along, my father was a guard on the Potomac Railroad, his father's own firm. The family business was thus kept in the family. According to my mother, he was making good money, eighteen dollars a week plus overtime and bonus when the company had a good year. The reason why he came to lose this wonderfully well-paid job that brought in so much money to enable us to fill our stomachs with corn bread and lard, and kill a chicken on christenings was never made clear. It seems this was the beginning of my father's earthly sorrows. With him our family fortunes had begun to decline. And as if fate took a malevolent hand, my mother's fertility increased in direct proportion to our mounting poverty. After my brother and me came three girls and two boys who literally ate everything in sight. My sisters, Lucille, Sharon and Dorothy (whom we call Dot for short), are all respectably married women now. Lucille is married to a man I know to be nothing but a racketeer, but in my family's vocabulary he is in real estate in Philadelphia. They move in high Negro Society, her husband now a pillar of the black community, a lay preacher, and a property owner. There was recent news that he was running for mayor as a coalition candidate, the unanimous choice of the Italian and black communities, the only person guaranteed to bring the races together in Philadelphia. My sister Lucille left home when she was sixteen, a sweet black-eyed beauty, to visit one of my aunts in Detroit. When I last saw her she was as fat as a paddock cow. She has not had children.

Sharon, my favorite, turned out good. She married a fellow who once upon a time pumped gas on the corner of our street. They moved west to San Francisco. We have reports that the guy has done well for himself. My sister and her kids, they say, are as happy as spring time bluejays. Sharon was close to me, maybe because she looked like my mother. Tall with bright brown eyes, long treselled hair like fields of corn, and high full cheeks. In fact she looked like Nefertiti, the Egyptian goddess, wife of King Akhnaten. And I knew she was Nefertiti when we were younger, the African goddess who has returned to earth in America among her suffering children locked here in Babylon. As kids Sharon and I used to roam our backyard and the valley for hours searched for groves and caverns, for the habitation of all the tall-tale animals of my mother's folk memory: brer rabbit and his cousins and the pranky squirrels.

I could trap bull finches and sparrows. We kept and nursed them playing father and mother to then. After I left home in 55, I heard the gas man who used to bring brown bags of groceries—my mother said they were stolen sure as the good Lord was in heaven—came and proposed to her. After a few months of linving in the little room behind the station, they both split and went westwards. Now they say he is a well-to-do dude in Frisco. I still carry a picture of my nephews—four boys. The eldest is named for me. They are strong healthy looking kids who will probably run for mayor of a black city or even become vice presidents of the United States one day before I move on.

And my sister Dot. She is a gas. She had the temper of eight tarantulas and an enormous heart of gold. My father was just not a lover of children like J. Christ, but Dot we were sure he positively hated. There were many days when the house was like a graveyard following a desperate fight between my parents over Dot. Come to think of it, she had no defender for her numerously confused causes except my mother, our safe stronghold. I was unashamedly indifferent towards her because she ignored me as much as she could. And I acted the big brother bully to her passionate personality. She lives in the Bronx now, working as a practical nurse in Montefiori Hospital. When I needed money a couple of occasions, I mean real bad, Dot rolled me two twenty dollar bills and a ten with a cry in her voice. When I shacked up in Harlem with the African Revolution boys for two years, in 67-69 I didn't see much of her.

My elder brother Kevin died in 59 in a senseless auto crash near Baltimore. Our two brothers Herb and Al, I haven't kept up with much. Herb played some basketball in high school, but couldn't win a scholarship to go to college. I guess it's because his basket wasn't too hot either. I don't think my family is very bright, period. Al is in some kind of federal program in DC training to become a housing officer in one of those new agencies founded to quieten black people down, going by such grand names like equal opportunity and urban renewal.

But you mustn't run away with the impression my family was never together or that we spent our waking hours tearing into one another until we went our several ways on the rambling face of this great democracy. No sir!! We had great moments of family unity, especially in those months in early 55, when father was ill with a cough that finally took him away in the early fall of that year. We used to hang out in the yard waiting for our mother's call to go in and pray for our father. He used to just lie there, his color ashy grey, his eyes bright, sharp and prominent waiting anxiously to read in our faces how much we cared and how long he would last on this earth. We loved him then, very much. And we felt our combined weakness in his dying. He tried to transmit some message of hope to us. But being a cynic himself, and having suffered so much, his message never came through except to me at last. We were united not so much by his imminent death, but by the overwhelming void that his coming absence would create in our midst. We were about to enter into that coming void, afraid and vulnerable. We had lost Christ somewhere along the line, I mean collectively. The girls still had him, but only in their secret and private lives. And it was in our father's approaching death that I, seventeen and ready, read the sad saga of the so-called Negro in this bitter land.

AT MY BIRTH, THERE MUST HAVE BEEN a dangerous star of affliction, a spirit of restlessness and wanderlust in the ascendancy. My infancy and early childhood were gloriously uneventful, and I will not invent any great episodes for the benefit of those of my readers who are sold on the myth that all Negro childhoods in America are bleak sorrowful affairs full of dispossession and despair. And I am not saying I had a great childhood either, except that to put it poetically, it was a long dreary and at times half-famished dreamy afternoon, with the sun eternally hanging in one place right above our house, now and then an alternating morning of Virginian rain, grey clouds, and open fields stretching into the woodlands beyond which other folks—white folks I presume—lived. And that was all I can remember.

But I must have begun to be aware of the world and my surroundings when I was six. There was one blighted winter day unusually cold, when the whole world was ablaze. We ran to the road which so long as I could remember always passed in front of our porch. In the skies were curly black clouds of smoke billowing in the heavens playing pranks with a few kites and buzzards drawn by curiosity. Soon my father came home, and as usual gingerly opened the door and ordered us all in. We spent that afternoon on our knees led by mother in prayer. Up till today, I do not remember what happened, but it seemed that that was the afternoon of my birth, the day I came of age, rejected God and religion, and proceeded to perceive and take in the world by my own light.

I was seventeen, long dropped out of high school, when my father died. His death was designed by him to be some kind of punishment for us. But it turned out differently. I hung around a few gangs, harmless groups of kids, trying to figure out what it was all about. That particular afternoon we had gone again to the railroad yard to fetch and carry. There wasn't much that day, so I guess we must have been sent away with about a dollar or two in our pockets by early afternoon. I was hanging out at the YMCA when my brother Kelvin who was working as a bellboy in a hotel downtown came and called me away. He was unusually silent. I sensed something had gone wrong at home. I knew Dad wasn't very well, but I particularly didn't care in my sullen rebelliousness whether he lived or died. He was my Dad all right, but we just never hit it together. Not that we ever exchanged more than a sentence before the sun set. He had withdrawn since he lost his job with the railroad company into a distant world of his own from where he censored our every behavior and move as calculated acts of defiance against him now that he had lost his eminent position as the principal breadwinner in the family. And that was ever since I was a child. My mother still kept her job as the cleaning lady in a research laboratory four miles out of town, and so we had some food and warmth in the winter. I was young and free, if even my adolescence looked blighted and dismally unheroic. I kept on blooming in my heart a bouquet of hope. I will ride out all my early youth of despair into a brave tomorrow when I will do things, make money by any means (that is the cardinal motto of our great nation), rise or fall by my own secret light. My father's illness had grown worse the past few days. He occupied the same position in the living room, winter or summer near a small fire kept on like the burning briars of a lingering diety. I was irritated to no end by the long time he took dying, by the space he occupied in our hearts, and the censorious silence with which he observed our every move. What manner of a man was he that he will take such a long messy time to die? Did he have none of his earlier sense of honor and pride left to enable him get it over with fast and leave us in peace? There was a gloom that had descended over our moderately happy household since he took ill. And it signified itself in a certain hushed anticipation of calamity that I hated with a silent passion. Why must our lives be blighted and our youth suspended because our father was dying? And besides, our mother's solicitous concern for the guy was an overbearing and frightful thing to behold. She stood by his arm-chair or bed whenever she was at home, a short tear in her eyes, anticipating every wish of his. And I suspected he rather enjoyed the attention in the very elaborate way he luxuriantly went about his eating and bathing. And in these otherwise ordinary daily affairs, I read a mystical ritual, a sacred ceremony at which my mother was the sad-eyed priestess performing a sacerdotal role for my father the diety. He had been ill since the early spring. It was now fall getting into winter. The richness of autumn and early winter and its brown somberness had descended upon the world. I always knew the secret messages of the seasons. I was said to be the poet of the family. This time of year always gives birth to sadness in my heart, its musty rotting vegetation and black trees erect in howling winds, reminders of an ancestral sorrow. Or perhaps I was always a sensitive boy, taken to too much grieving over things that others may find to be trivial. Or perhaps I had embarked upon a long road of secret understanding that will goad me on into rebellion against the established order of those who cannot see and hear. So what of it, if my poetry was not so much joy and celebration, if it expressed itself in vengeful withdrawals and long drawn bouts of self-pity? I know and live this sorrow always, and will till I die. But it was that late fall that I drew closer to my father. Our two wills fought continuously over what, now looking back, seems a series of inconsequential arguments. Looking back now, how much I did resemble him in his smouldering agony and silent suffering! I had never courted his favors as my elder brother Kelvin always did. I had never sought from him that familiar bond they say links father and son. And the newfound love and unity was not mine alone. It was for all of us. But I hated the prayers and the visit of the preacher who was nothing but a lying vulgarian feeding fat on other people's deeply felt sorrow. He would come in on Sunday afternoons, spouting inane pieties and quotations from the Bible. We the children were all united in our imminent loss. And we resented the way he spoke to us, reminding us, me in particular, of our duties to Christ and the church that kept our ancestors alive in a strange land. His carryings on about the Good Lord we found irritating and patently unfeeling, calculated insults to my sense of independence. Where was the Good Lord when we needed him? Where was He hiding when we tottered on a collective verge of annihilation? Talk of the birds of the air and lilies of the field toiling not and yet having a bountiful time of it. What about us, the ones he created they say in his own image? What did we do wrong to be condemned to an eternity of suffering in other people's vineyard? And my father lay there in his father's bed, scarcely forty-five, racked by cancer and dying in front of his wife and children. And we were being enjoined every Sunday by this sanctimonious leech to keep our eyes on the Good Lord and His convenant with His children!

By the time we reached our aged porch, I knew father was dead. Our house was not the newest in the Negro section of town. It was built by my grandfather who was one of the earliest Negroes to acquire a two-acre plot when the whites, under pressure from the Virginia State legislature, agreed to sell land to them late last century. The section itself was nondescript, not the most glamourous land on the western slope of the hills. But it overlooked a long endless valley that swept as far as the eyes could see, terminating in a misty hill over fifteen or so miles away. On this hill are now perched a series of new projects, all glisteningly white, the suburbia created by white refugees who are these days abandoning the cities to us. And there was wood in this valley. And water. A few farmers still hired occasional labor when the potato harvest was on. A couple of black folks owned more than ten acres, which is a hell of a lot, and raised crops such as corn and peanuts. We supplied occasional labor on these farms as boys, but because they didn't pay well, we always moved on to white farms where we could make a penny or so more in whatever task we were engaged. But we loved our valley.

A dirt road once upon a time passed in front of our house. By the time I left it was tarred and cars used to whiz past like demons hell bent. We were no longer exactly on the outskirts of town. But we were not downtown either. Growth and decay had reached us. Perhaps it was not new in our midst, death I mean. It had stalked us down the centuries snatching us once in a while in a benevolent act of salvation from our collective degradation, slapping our wrists in moments of rebellion against our allotted destiny. But it remained a staunch ally, giddy, hollow-eyed, full of jokes and laughter at our wakes, drunken, irreverent and disorderly the mornings after, but riding along with us, the guard and centurion of our hapless legions locked here in Babylon. He was always a friend in his solicitous concern for our ultimate integrity achieved only in his abode. For what serves a million proclamations, a million marchers on Washington? We would be told we were making progress in this hothouse of racism. That we too will finally win a place in the sun, where our color would no longer serve as our badge of defect even though it is always the malignant and malevolent insignia of our niggerhood.

That afternoon, my father died. He must have died a few minutes before we arrived on our ancient porch. There was an eerie silence, a silence loudly proclaimed by the sweet smell of death. It was the scented smell of funeral parlors and mortuaries. My mother sat in the old rocking chair, bright-eyed, silent and larger now than life. It seemed as if she had finally achieved a victory; silence became her last refuge. My sisters were scattered in the room around the eating table, weeping silently. The boys, in their green age, were perhaps not very keenly aware of the nature of our collective loss. My mother asked us to go in and say good-bye to our father. I paused at the entrance to his and my mother's room, unable to figure out exactly my expectations. He lay on his bed in his bath robe and pajamas. His hands were neatly folded upon his chest. I was sure he did this himself before dying. He looked shrivelled and dried up, his arms wound into bulging veins. His eyes were closed. But there was something proud and haughty about him, something which resembled a last minute defiance playing around his full lips and his nostrils. In life he was a man full of disdain for lesser men, a man who carried his pride like an ancestral heirloom, ready to flaunt his independence and sense of freedom in the face of any weakling. But he too had known the bitter taste of failure which even though it did not diminish the grandeur of his liberty, dulled the sharp edge of his scorn for those who did not possess his nobility. He must have been a lonely man, plagued by a secret memory of things long done and perhaps only vaguely forgotten. He did not see people as people in a gigantic complex system, manipulable to destruction. He saw them as creatures in charge of their own private destinies, and who, in spite of the public and collective nature of their sorrow and suffering, must rise up in their individual secret souls, and march on in spite of the planned infirmities of race.

Mother sent us to go back to town to tell Mr. Herbert the undertaker to come for father. That evening, in the quickening fall night, I drew closer to my father. That secret memory became mine. What amazed me most was that I was not aware of the burning rage that shattered his being everyday of his life, the incredible will that drove him to death rather than survive physically as food for sorrow. His death was heroic suicide in my eyes. The man saw the nature of the struggle, and chose death. He must have been responsible for the loss of his job, might have literally begged to be fired, and when he was, he carried his heart in his hands, came home among those whom in his own way he loved in order to die. And his death was my birth.

I seemed to be more aware of the world then. My senses of smell, touch, and taste became keener. I began to take a close look at people, at the world. My heart began to stir from a deep slumber of four centuries. I was seventeen, free, and newly born into a wild field of new sensations. But where do I turn? Where can I go? I was not aware of any tangible course of action open to me. I was not even aware of a choice. But I was aware of my mind and senses. I was aware of the historical wilderness in which I and my people had lived. Something surged in me, a power billowing in a million waves of indescribable strength as I watched my father's face in ashen death. The funeral was simple the way he wished. A few forgotten relatives, uncles and aunts, came from North Carolina, a nondescript horde of sad and mildly sorrowing people. They came, wept for a day and a half and vanished on the evening of the second day into their anonymous worlds. They made no impressions on us. A couple of the women fussed. The men sat aloof smoking some cheap and foul-smelling cigars bought from corner bars, and muttering in their mustaches as they gave us the boys advice on life. I ignored them as much as I could. I was in a new world, in the throes of new sensations. I was discovering myself and my potentialities. My father had died so that I might be saved. How ironic? I, who never cared much for him, who considered him a proud bullying silent intruder, the man who had been in my way all the days of my life? How was it possible for me to dwell in a new body through his death, to become someone else destined for great journeys beyond his wildest imaginings? Indeed, there was a bond that tied us together and I was the one who never knew it. But he knew. Always. And he planned it all for me. I was the one he loved and cared about most. I was the one on whom he focused his being, his hopes for collective salvation,. But why did he never talk to me about these deep and satisfying matters of the soul? Why did he not consciously prepare me for the role he had written out for me? The more I thought about it, the more I drew nearer to him in death.

As I said, the funeral was short, denied the howling aura of the organized hysteria that always marked the funerals of our people. One or two of my aunts from afar wept most copiously. But they were strangers, and we did not care if strangers cried at my father's funeral. We, the children and my mother, as if by an agreement, did not shed a tear. Maybe we felt a vicarious relief that the man was at last dead, or that he was free at last as the old spiritual said. But we were not burdened by the grief that opens up floodgates of tears. By his death we were aware that the unity of our household was over. As a family we would go our several ways, the girls will get married, and my mother ... My mother! It is as if there had been the conclusion that she would collect the pieces of her life and remain with us forever. How much we take for granted about those we love! Had I not, the beloved of my mother, forgotten her already in the exhiliration of my new-found strength? What was to become of her? I did not know, nor did I honestly want to think about it.

The funeral was behind us. I couldn't cope with the quietude that surrounded me after it. I wanted to escape, to flee, fly away into the vastness of this land, lose myself. But how?

Exactly six months after I left home, I was in jail.

AND FOR ONE HUNDRED AND TEN DAYS by my count we plodded through the savanna. The grass scarcely came to our breast as we followed a long trail made by earlier feet on our march towards the coast. The dead were buried in shallow graves on the edge of the narrow desert of our travail. Our road led southwards following the arch of the sun.

Before us the country spread, a field of grey clouds overlooking an eternity of brown grass. There were a few trees or clumps of bushes in this new wilderness, bustling giants of gaunt palms, thrusting out in their solitary sorrow, sweeping with the branches against the widening skies. Our days opened with the cold chill of the blowing northern wind, dry and parched, having driven us into huddled retreats in which we sought each other's warmth for survival. The days hung on our march, saturated with sorrow and the sweat of the noon dripping from our glistening bodies. Time itself, immeasurable and hollow, was suspended in the cavernous echo of the empty heavens beneath which we traced our steps. Weariness was unpardonable. But we carried a surprisingly wondrous buoyancy of spirit, especially at those indistinct hours of enduring brightness when our jubilant flesh proclaimed our humanity. Our nakedness made us one with the air, the wind and the tree. It was the only thing we needed to repossess our souls after moments of lapsing forgetfulness. In the brief darkness of conscious nights, the task was the renewal of the spirit, the bracing of the intimate self. Otherwise what way else could we have retained our inheritance as we proceeded on that journey into the grim un-

known? We were the proprietors of our only ultimate truths, the tearful worshippers at our own shrines, supplicants before resigned deities.

Within the lengthening days that moved into more lengthening months, perishing moments in which we carried the smell of the land in our noses, some of the infants wept continuosly, offering a cacophonous chorus to our ordeal. Their music accompanied us like a long forgotten tribal dirge sung before the first burial. The earth, the only reality of contact, as our naked feet hit her in a silent processional unto death and degradation, numb to our senses. To us, the allegory and the tale of wandering was to become the final truth. We remained shrouded in a film of dust receiving only the harsh grating intonation of light, which as we went south began to acquire patches of brilliance and color. Turbulent winds rose, promising storm and rain that never came. Now riding gently in the dust, the northern wind, which others call the author of quick silent death at night, would be the horse relieving our feet of weariness. But she carried with her the unannounced acquaintanceship of death, inexorable and instant. To many, it did not matter if we died then. The distance repeated itself a million times, the grassland rolling ahead of us for days, weeks and months.

One day, we arrived in an abandoned settlement. It could not have been deserted long before we came. The round conical houses were still intact. There were a few granaries now empty of grain. It looked as if the villagers left in a desperate hurry, as if an instant calamity broke upon them one noon, and they fled southwards into the impenetrable unknown. As our captors led us through the village, we smelt something distantly familiar about it. A few huts on the outskirts were still smouldering. Our procession led to the centre of the village where an ancient shrine stood. The sun was red in the west, and it seemed the plan was to camp here for the night. Our rank had been depleted by death. We were halted near the shrine, and the order given to pause. Scarcely had we settled down when an eerie sound hit our ears, a sharp prolonged ulula-

tion announcing calamity. Our captors jumped upon their feet, their machetes ready. The sound came from right behind us. Our eyes were trained upon the little shed beside the shrine, covered with grass mats which had almost rotted. And soon, as if summoned by our apprehension and collective fear, an apparition appeared.

It was human, seeing that it walked on two feet. Her eyes (it turned out to be a woman as she came nearer) were as brown as the earth on which she walked. Her total nakedness was disguised with a few leaves covering her privacy. Her breasts were long limp straps, drooping unto her belly. There was something wild and unbelievable about her, a look sublime in fact, that carried a passion of lunacy beyond description. Her strides were swift, determined and measured, in their aggressive thrust towards where we all, captors and captives, now stood. There was something sinister in her approach, something that revealed a hidden story without words. She bore on her face the marks of the regions through which we had been traveling, long tiny but thick marks that covered her whole countenance. There was a deep impenetrable aura about her, revealed more in her earthy eyes. Her cries, it seemed, were more of groans interlarded with wild screams. Her breath heaved in gallops towards an ultimate release. Her maniacal wails rose and fell in a frenzy of waves terminating now in a low moan, and now rising into a shrill, crashing crescendo of unhuman sounds. It was not easy to tell in what private hell she was, and how more private it was than ours. Our band, travel-weary, was all alert now witnessing this re-enactment of our own sorrow.

When it looked as if she would collapse amoung us, as she had picked up speed, she abruptly halted. She scanned our faces, her left palm over her brow. Her eyes proved not to be brown, but red, redder than the earth. They were ablaze with an indescribable fire. As she stared into our souls, transfixed us with her gaze, she remained still. One of our captors made as if he would move. And as sudden as lightning, the woman or rather the apparition for that was what she was, raised her right arm into a striking position. This gesture was accompanied by a shrill cry, not an ululation as before, but the cry of a wounded animal caught in the grinding teeth of a primeval trap. She now confronted the man who had made the move. For an eternity they stared at each other, she holding him in her eyes, sizing him up, tearing his very being apart in order to reach his deepest recesses. Her eyes were not accusing eyes, but boring and querying asking questions which she knew perhaps could not be answered. After an eternity of this confrontation, she raised here eyes to heaven, shifted her gaze upon the empty skies, blue and inexorable, as if calling down the visitation of powers and forces that can parley with her. In that instant, a song rose up on her lips. It began as a deep gurgling ramble in her throat. It was more a prayer than a song. Perhaps a hymn to a deity. Her gaze was still on the sky as she moved among us, slowly, raising one foot after the other; we stood still overawed by this moment of dream in which this phantom had invaded our silent sorrow. What was she? Where did she come from? It looked to us as if this village had been subjected to a raid just before our arrival. The smouldering fires of the burning huts witnessed it. And it seemed that this woman phantom or spirit was the only survivor of the carnage and the destruction. All the others might have been captured and led away in chains as we were. Men, women and children led on the leash, jangling their way down the grass, the forest and to the sea. And what was the purpose of this lone survivor's prayer? She moved among us, her hands outstretched before her. We stood still, gripped by an untold sense of imminent doom. Very soon, her song turned into a shrill cry, and she had begun to sob uncontrollably. She lowered her eyes from the heavens and started to touch everyone in her way. She touched some of us in the face. Her touch was a gentle caress that lingered on the chin and then moved to the cheeks, the eyebrow, the forehead and the hair. She continued to sing softly as she moved from man to man, from woman to child. We the captives were in a state of paralyzed fascination. Her touch was soothing. It was the act of a mother bathing and preparing her baby for an outdooring. Some of the women started to cry, and even the infants overwhelmed perhaps by the silence of this ritual and benediction, were raising an infernal din.

Our captors stood aside, watching. At first they were astonished by the unexpected appearance of the woman. They had proposed to move in and drive her off. But soon they too were overpowered by the apparitional force. They stood completely immobile, watching. A look of utter consternation was on the face of the others when the woman stood up in defiant challenge to one of them. Their power as captors was momentarily forgotten; they had resigned that which they had exercised over us throughout our journey. As the phantom proceeded on her promenade among us, and caressed our faces with her feeble hands and gentle fingers, our captors' surprise became deepened. She was now among the women and children. Her song was now a low moan. And just as she reached the last woman, she turned suddenly as if bitten by an insect and with both her arms raised began to move towards our captors. She was screaming now. It sounded as if she was uttering curses, voluble, swift and loud, at these men as she marched towards them. The hyenas had fear on their faces, and were clutching their machetes and ready to do battle. She continued her determined march upon them. Just as she reached the first man, the same man she had confronted earlier, she jumped upon him grappling with him with all her strength. Both fell to the ground in a cloud of dust.

Suddenly everyone came to life. We the captives had also woken up from our state of trance. But because of our chains we could not move. The woman was still in the dust. Machetes flashed in the air as our captors went into battle. Two men were over her hacking away at her body. It was like the scene at a primordial hunt, the hunters cutting at the dying animal. All this took a very short time, like ten blinkings of the eye. It was over. The phantom woman or spirit or what remained of her lay in a bloody heap. Her head had almost been severed at the back of the neck. Her body—arms and chest—was gashes of red wounds oozing blood. She was still alive, as the trunk continued to jerk, to beat a rhythmic tattoo upon the red earth now soaked with blood. Silence had descended upon us once more. The crumpled body continued to heave, jerk, rise and fall with its dying breath. We all stood watching. Our captors had moved away from it, perhaps more impelled by fear and disbelief. The woman's caresses were still on our faces, her eyes still upon ours, her voice still in our ears. The body took an eternity dying, and at the moment it died, the camp came to life again. Orders went out that we must rise and depart. We could not spend the night here. Our captors were anxious to leave the scene of their fear.

The night had deepened around us and this drama of death. There was something vaguely subliminal about it perhaps because she was a phantom and we were real. We had all, I suppose, wished for this act of violence and death to be enacted before our eyes in spite of our chains. It did not exactly achieve a purgation in our souls, but it released our long manacled spirits and set them soaring in the knowledge that this perhaps was the ultimate end of our journey. We were not given to fury, pity or indignation, but a deep and silent hysterical joy that what had looked complex and complicated had been untangled neatly in a resolution of a simple act of violence and death. The allegory had become the truth, a monstrously dramatic truth that affirmed for us the purpose of our onward journey. Our circles of death had been widened, and the march must go in. We had tasted the invisible drink of truth; though we shuddered in the embrace of this truth, our names had been written down at last. Some, unlike the poet, were not aware of the prophetic essence of the drama; others had not abandoned hope in the search for gratuitous miracles. So into the moonlight we stumbled in a frenzied march against the cold of the har-

mattan, our flesh peeling in goose pimples, emaciated by the blistering agony of the journey. I was the only one whose blood had enjoined him to keep watch over the tribe, for that was what we had become in the unity of spilt blood, the only tribe we shall ever know. My vow was not to become oblivious of this blood that would bear us, like the mounting wave of survival, from defeat to defeat (or was it victory?) and lead us home. In that blood is encapsulated the poison in the being of the bird and the beast, the blast of the plant in its denudation while it crackled and smoked under the furious assault of the bird and the beast. There would be a light, incandescent, trembling in the blazoning flowers that would lead us on.

I SAID IN SIX MONTHS, I WAS IN JAIL. But this is only to mean the formal incarceration that follows the free roaming landscape of our historical prison. (We had freedom, since Emancipation, freedom to die of hunger, to rot in the blue nights of urban despair, to die in the sweet embrace of our Anglo-Saxon matron Liberty, the woman in the harbor, carrying the burning torch).

Duke P. Smith, our neighborhood hero, tough-minded lover of freedom and liberty, twice jailed for petty crimes such as holding up gas stations and attempted murder (endowed he is with a terror of a temper) was leaving for New York. And that is north of my Virginian hometown. And because it was north, it wore the miraculous garb of the unreal city of redemption. I was young and still retained the possibility of being on the verge of great things. I too must go north.

We hit the road three nights after the last funeral guest had left town. My mother had accepted the inevitability of my departure; she had become resigned to the sorrow of the break up of our home. That was the ultimate truth that followed our father's death. It was late fall, the browning of trees, the golden riot of the plants and shrubs of Virginia. Duke handled his 1949 Dodge like an army handling a riot. We drove through mazes of lights, small towns asleep on the edge of somnolent farms. We stopped for gas a couple of times, and just to enable Duke rest his eyes, we sat on little curbs and talked of our hopes. Duke was about twenty. But as I said, he had done time twice already. He was a well developed lad with a barrel chest out of which rolled the deepest voice I've ever heard. He was not very tall, but carried a lot of strength and vitality in his medium-sized frame. There was a restlessness about him, a melancholic refusal to accept his fate as an orphan. His mother died young in childbirth, and his father was brought home from the sawmill on the edge of town completely smashed up by some monstrous machine a year later. Duke was about eight.

He ran away from the county orphanage and hitch-hiked to North Carolina where he claimed he had had an aunt. When he returned from his travels to the South seven years later, he was already a man of the world at fifteen. He knew about survival, sex and the ethics upon which Babylon was built. So he became our neighborhood hero and leader. He hired himself out at the Odeon, a noisy smelly roach-infested cinema house expressly built for niggers. It was run by old Tom Delawney, a pot-bellied consumptive ex-serviceman who had spent his life in the army and the war guarding an ammunition depot somewhere in Texas. He was like a father to Duke. There was a relationship that bordered on a conspiracy between these two. Duke earned enough to keep himself in clothes and acquire a twenty-five year old divorcee as his girl friend. Betty Lou was not exactly pretty; her mouth was too long, but she was every adolescent boy's wet dream in a malnourished black farming community. She was generous, and liberally endowed with motherly instincts. It was on account of her that Duke one day nearly committed murder. A truck driver from Milwaukee had picked Betty Lou up one night in the Swing Corner Bar and was heading towards the trailer camp on the edge of town when Duke drove up in a noisy Chevrolet he was putting together in those days. The truck driver was carried to Stintson Memorial Hospital (for Negroes) where he received exactly fifteen stitches on his head.

It's otherwise that when niggers kill niggers, the law doesn't much bother. But Duke's attempted murder was done in full view of three leading white Baptist families who were very much concerned with the spread of Negro violence. When Duke came out of jail, he was already a man of eighteen. He sported a smart beard and a knowing smile in his eyes. Everyday he spoke haltingly of moving north. Tom Delawney was dead when he came back. So he was pretty much left on his own, doing odd jobs here and there. He had acquired an advanced but indifferent skill in auto mechanics while he was in jail. But the community couldn't hold him no more. Betty Lou had drifted westwards. Some guys claimed to have seen her in San Diego, others in Phoenix. We the kids still admired Duke and he provided in his quiet unspoken way, his undying leadership and inspiration.

That night, driving all the way to New York with Duke, I heard him say more than he had ever said in his whole short life. I was seventeen. I still nourished in my heart a desperate hope that would break open for me the magic doors of achievement. I had dropped out of high school, not because I was not bright enough to sustain the discipline of study. I left because it all looked like a dreary dusty road which led to nowhere but to little errand boy and back-breaking jobs in white establishments. I was ready for the world, but the world was not ready for me. And so I decided to force her attention and readiness, force her to accept my talents, and to turn me around, to fulfill me. I was not yet aware of the infinite disabilities that rose like mirages of fate on my journey, as they tried hard to learn me the knowledge of my history and the legends of my race. But who says a Negro boy born in the dirt patches of Virginia cannot demand a hearing from the world's court of conscience? My freedom was wrapped in my few clothes, and in the historical talisman of color worn like the Jews wore the Star of David. But mine was more available for viewing than theirs. That night I listened to Duke as he spoke volubly outlining his private intimate dreams. He had this friend he met in jail, a guy who now lived in Brooklyn. This guy, see, had secured him a job with a garage that would pay him the unheard of wage of one and a half dollars per hour for just greasing cars, changing oil, and fixing tyres. I ain't hoping for too much, man, he said. But man, like I know what's going to happen out there. Like this cat, Mel, the cat I met in jail, usta say, there ain't nothing, no rap out there that you can't beat if you just get out and be your own man. Like that time when my mother passed away, I could've given all up and gone, man, just gone down. But hell, who's to tell you can't fix it all up and strike out. And Mel was a white dude, a white Jew dude from Brooklyn who told me to take a trip. I was surprised that his friend Mel was a white man. But if I had known what jail was I wouldn't be surprised. There was another dark force behind Duke's words that darkening and lengthening fall night as we sped towards the city of god. I felt a warm glow in my heart that this demon of a man, this dreamer had agreed to accept the companionship of a man-child. He always used to say I was a poet on account of how I put things. That I had a magic way with words as I wove them on my tongue into little circlets of gold, jewelled crowns that will yet be our salvation. Duke said, one day when we are in trouble and are hauled before the devil, I would make those words dance before the man and so effect our release. But, I, being the poet, was also aware that Duke was my other self. His silent strength was the seat of my real strength. I was still in my teens, even though death and sickness had made an early home in my heart. I knew of sorrow by instinct. She was my kinswoman. In Duke was that resolution of will, that uncrumbling "Negro" will to survive on its long drawn and melancholy journey.

When we hit the New Jersey Turnpike, Duke said we were

almost home. The road sped on, through flat marshlands, the greying lights of early dawn breaking out there behind us now and now to our right. The old Dodge held steadily at a breakneck seventy-five miles an hour, now and then shuddering, trembling like a victorious race horse. Duke sure could handle the beast, caressing her now, and now whipping it into action. He had built it all from an old decrepit abandoned car into this beautiful brute that still retained its pristine power. Beyond the Delaware Memorial Bridge, our road was now straight towards New York. Full dawn was on us when we entered the Lincoln Tunnel. New York was still asleep on a grey morning as we crossed the city heading for the west side highway. A glow settled upon me that morning on seeing the legendary city for the first time. Someday I will describe that glow and its inspiration. It stayed with me for a long time, even the pain of prison could not wipe it away from my heart. From the west side we hit the Brookyn Bridge that led us slowly into Atlantic Avenue, one of those arterial boulevards of Brooklyn. Duke had written a close description of our route as he learned it from Mel. Atlantic Avenue is one of those never-ending streets sweeping from a wide two-lane avenue into a trappy route underneath an overhead railroad, unwinding steadily into the distant suburbia of Queens. As we rode on, it was as if, having come to the end of our journey, the possibility of wandering without halting had become very real. And a cloud seemed to hang on Duke's face. After what must have been an hour, the man confessed we were lost. At this he pulled up into a curb and we laughed our first laugh in the big apple. Maybe we laughed because we had come to the dividing line of our lives' journey. We were shedding, like the snake, the shrouds of our southern infancy and agonized youth. It was almost preposterous that here we were lost in a strange city, and we were laughing like a pair of imbeciles into a cavernous dawn. We were not bothered by the unfamiliarity of our surroundings. We were laughing at the extended joke which marked our lives. There was still some winged hope flying and fluttering in our bosoms. For, in this strange city we were ready to sing our personal hymns without fear. Our mirth that morning was like the ringing slogans of faith proclaimed by demented priests and believers. Encircled by the aroma of indistinct strangers, we yielded to the hilarity that seemed to have shielded us all along. But it was not the mirth of the vanquished nor of evening. It was the mirth of a coming victory and a new morning, what the poet saw as poised for great revelations. Perhaps it was a cover for our doubts, for the maddening grief that lurked in the corridors of our lives.

After a phone call, we drove to Mel's apartment on Essex Street in the New Lots section of Brooklyn. A sad-eyed, sallow Jew of an indeterminate age opened the door for us at 5:30 A.M. We sank into a pile of lumpy chairs. While Duke and Mel exchanged news of mutual friends and of their time in a Virginian jail, I slipped off into a long peaceful sleep which must have lasted for a day. For, when I woke up, it was around the same hour. Meg and Duke were still swapping stories, filling in the blanks of their mutual memories.

New York, April 5, 1956. This is the city of sirens. I heard them in the streets as the revolving lights of cop cars cast long shadows on my opposite wall. I was still asleep because I was on a night shift in a plastics factory in New Hyde Park further on the island. The job was not very heavy, and the money was not bad. Duke was with Mel in a well-known garage on Flatbush Avenue. He was happy and optimistic. I had picked up a few clothes to replace the boyhood outfit in which I came to the city. The routine of work was at times killing but the city was big and there was so much we could do especially on those delirious weekends when we played the gram and drank a pint of gin and apple juice. The winter had been cold but not unexpected. There were times when the cold was relentless and venomous, but it was we who had made the journey, and we were willing to undergo the initiation. Christmas that year was a cheerless festival, the first ever I spent away from home. But it was amazing how much I had grown, in fact matured. My seventeen years and a few months were hidden behind a tall(six feet one) slightly stooped body, a small beard that had started coming since I turned sixteen. I knew I would have to survive in New York, and if I did, vindicate the wisdom of my flight from Virginia. The nagging doubt that I was still a youth, which had accompanied me to New York, had receded. In its place was a newly found sense of confidence which hid the fumbling and searching needs of my young days. Duke and I had not exactly drifted apart, but his world was more part of Mel's idealism. It was focused on things that were perhaps not immediately available to me, things which I could not understand. But I still roomed with them, the younger companion who now and then did the errands and fetched the beer. We still talked about the conditions of our souls and our destiny. Mel was the first white man I saw at close quarters, and I was astonished. At first I exhibited towards him that confused temerity that marks the life of most black southern youth. Our world and that of white folks never actually met. We sensed the already existing barriers when we were barely old enough to look after ourselves. They were demonstrated to us in our parents' oblique references to white folks and the need for us children to watch our steps and trust in the good Lord. We were vaguely aware of the powerful forces that defined us and them. In our mythology and legends there are sad and tearful stories of men lynched for sneezing while a white lady was close by, and of many family heads gunned down for being sassy to the man. I didn't understand the bond that bound Mel and Duke. Mel's folk, he one day told us, were immigrants from eastern Europe. They came right after the first world war. They were still somewhere in New Jersey. He was an only son. His father ran a shoe repair shop. He left home after his barmitzvah and headed for New York. There he got a job as a mail truck driver, until on one drunken weekend in Richmond (where he had gone to see his gal) he ended up in jail, found guilty of assault and causing grievous bodily harm to some redneck jerk who had insulted him. Mel was a dreamer. He did not now care very much whether anyone called him names. There was something simple or almost holy about him. This I found later to be his enormous humanity in an inhuman world.

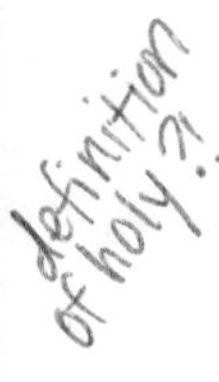

I was still lying on my cot in the living room. It was sometime between five and six. I was keeping my eye on the clock that had woken me up at five. I would have to catch a bus at 5:45 that would take me to New Hyde Park around six-thirty. My work at the factory started at 7 P.M. I was not fully awake. I hovered between sleep and waking. Suddenly I heard the door bell ring. I was in half a mind not to go to the door. The area had been besieged by an army of salesmen, persistent peddlers of goods of indeterminate quality. I stretched out more, hoping that whoever was ringing would go away. After a short pause came a loud knock, a cross between a thumping and an attempt to break down the door. I gathered my bed clothes around me and made for the door. After unlatching the chain and removing the iron bar that went by the grand name of a police lock, I looked through the spy glass. All I saw was a blur which finally merged into a white face in which two bluish-grey eyes penetratingly fixed their gaze on the spy glass. I turned the key releasing the last lock. The door flew open because the man outside had pushed it and had already sprung into the room. I will not repeat the conversation that took place. The upshot of it was that I was handcuffed in my sleeping clothes and led to a waiting car in which sat two other men, their faces perfect studies of that unhealthy brutality which the average policeman carries with him. I asked the man who arrested me to tell me my crime. But he just kept silent, hostility in his now perfectly grey eyes. Panic seized me. What had I done? My mind raced over the past six months since I came to the city. By instinct I was a law abiding person. I did not even know the laws, but I carried within me a rudimentary dislike of what may constitute an illegality. My parents were not exactly disciplinarians, but they had instilled in me a simple-minded respect for the brutality that the law of our rulers represented. So my mind raced over the past six months, and I came to the conclusion that I was an innocent man. A little lamp of joy and inner peace lit in my heart once I knew I was innocent. I turned round and looked at my captors. There was venom in their eyes. My prospective jailers were not aware of my humanity. I was to them only part of the statistics of urban crime, an object of their dutiful attendance to their profession, black, inexorable, as sure as sin and my Baptist hereafter. But let me not prejudge anything.

The car sped through town till we arrived at a police precinct somewhere in the maze of Brooklyn. I was shoved into a cell and a door locked after me. Before I even had time to think and to adjust my mind to the situation, the door snapped open again; a police officer ordered me out. I stood behind the desk as my fingerprints were taken, my photograph taken, and a long sentence read to me. I was not too sure whether I heard the voice, but it droned on in its sleepy dull monotony about a hold-up on 86th Street and Third Avenue in Manhattan on March 8. I had held up a grocery store at gunpoint and made off with cash amounting to five hundred and eighty dollars. In the holdup I had assaulted and wounded the store owner who was still unconscious in a hospital somewhere in the city.

That same evening I was arraigned before a district judge

a pale looking, dark-haired Italian who never for once looked into my face as he read the charge, and recommended that I be held in Rikers Island jail. He placed bail at 15,000 dollars. I was returned to the cells where I spent the night on a cement slab without beddings, a pillow, and without food. Do not misunderstand me. I have the basic intelligence that makes me aware of my own responsibilities, fears, and expectations as a black man in America. That night, for the second time since the death of my father and the birth of my new personality I was afforded the occasion to rethink my personal destiny.

On the next morning I was driven by bus, with other youths, some younger, some older, to Rikers Island. Those of you who haven't heard of this island must look for it behind the narrow strip of water that almost encircles LaGuardia Airport. You cannot tell the size of this island if you are a prisoner on it. When the gates closed after me that noon, my mind jumped back to the past twenty four hours.

It did not seem, looking back on those hours, that I was destined to arrive at where I did. The previous day was a regular one, nothing spectacular. I came home just around six A.M. after my nine-hour shift overseeing a plastic moulding machine for accurate gauge, and switching controls from heat to cool every nine minutes. There wasn't anything spectacular about this job. It is the paid drudgery on which our nation survives. But for some of us these jobs are the only gateways to personal sanity. We would never become executives in suit in these establishments. I rode back on the regular bus, slower at the early dawn, and slid into our apartment on Essex Street. I ate a hurried meal of something the other guys left on the stove and slipped into my cot. I have always loved sleeping at late dawn; an early morning chill seeps through to me and my soul curls up into a neat little bundle. Most of my dreams occur at dawn, serving as cleansers for my mind. Perhaps because my morning sleeps were short. That morning I dreamt I was back at home. My father was alive, but he looked different. He looked more filled out, as he reclined in his favourite arm-chair, humming one of those little old blues tunes he loved so much. The hour was twilight, the skies darkening. My mother and sisters were all in the living room. It seemed as if the boys had not yet been born. There was an indescribable joy on the face of my father as he moved from song to song. Soon he was humming a spiritual. I didn't know what I myself was doing. There was deathly calm. My father's voice could be heard now as if it came from afar. It was one of those dirge-like spirituals. Suddenly below the song I heard the slow heavy thumping of many feet. Soon followed the jingling of bells. No. It was the jangling of chains. The two sounds became blended, fused into an indistinct yet rhythmic beat from out of the front yard. I rushed out to see and hear this funeral music. It was a procession on its way to the cemetery. But there was no hearse, no coffin. It was all men, half-naked at the top, moving slowly in two lines. A hymn, low and deep, emanated from this unreal procession of mourners on the way to the cemetery. But where was the corpse? A woman leading the procession carried a wrapped up bundle which she clutched to her bosom.

Suddenly, the procession changed into a chain gang in brown, striped, short jumpers. Around it was deathly silence, deep impenetrable silence. These men, dark, with faces hooded by the night, moved in a ghostly unison. Their chains jangled in a strange music that provided a far background to my father's now rising solo.

Then I was among them, chains on my hands and feet. I was part of the music of the chains, of the slow march that winded up the litlle-hill from the valley in front of our house.

Then my father's voice became fainter and fainter, as if it was fleeing away far now above us, indistinct. Only its melancholic note lingered on as we proceeded slowly into the deep night. I heard the opening of doors far away, an alien voice called my name.

When I woke up, it was evening in my cell. Soon the guards herded us all into a vast hall. We sat at tables scattered all over this cavernous hall. I lifted my head and looked around the vast hall. There must have been over one thousand of us in that wide room. Boys, stringy boys in their nervous adolescence, black boys, Puerto Ricans, and a few white boys, the young herd of the net lost generation. They seemed not to be aware of the trapdoor that had shut upon them. Perhaps some did not at seventeen care any more what happened to them, into what early nightmare they were being ushered.

I went back into my cell and cried. And it was the first day.

FIRST WE SAW IT AS A RISING MIST curled into the setting sun. Birds, white collared crows, were whirling like flags of a victory regiment on parade. Their festival swoops were a mockery to our beaten and shattered march. This crow energy in the face of death was the eloquent testimony to the flight of our human passions long washed away, and to our hollow world a testament of an enduring power now beyond us. But there was still in our hearts an eagled desire which knew no bounds. Perhaps in the impenetrable darkness before us, sorrow, that companion spirit of our fate, was no longer a sharpened sensibility, no longer the frenzied howl that would bestow on us the apprehension of a hired wayfarer in need of water. And so we journeyed on into the forest of our abandonment.

It had first appeared on the horizon, announced by the crows, crashing sudden at the tip of the sun into our yellowing eyes. The very earth had begun to smell different. Emanating from it a blue mist in which the birds cavorted hunting in the jubilee of light and rays. Like a herd of crouching animals, it heaved in the feeding gestures against the sun's march and the clouds' gambol.

Night was upon us when we entered the forest only to be assailed by a thick impenetrable darkness thickened by tall trees whose canopies covered our skies and the eyes of the heavens. Beneath our weary feet was a soft carpet of rotting leaves. A magic smell of mould and decay rose everywhere.

We camped near the first giant tree for the night. The night was a whining long moan of trees as they whispered in the periodic winds that rushed through the few lingering patches of cleared ground. We managed a few fitful winks of sleep punctuated by neighborly nightmares of screams and wild speech. It had been the same every night of our journey.

The rising of the sun began with tiny specks of distinguishable dust dancing on the leaves of the low shrubs. Soon long shafts of light white and shiny appeared in an army falling upon the brown leaf-covered earth. The columns of light played on the lower shrubs on our bodies and in our souls for a brief while; then they turned into giant monsters of watch that hovered over us the whole morning. The order was given to move on.

The giant trees reached almost to the heavens. Tall erect their bases were large ominous temples of marching feet that supported shrines and homes of gods and spirits. From the heavens their crowns dropped occasional dew and twigs. Several climbers clung upon their bodies like beads on the devotees of a god. Lichens and epiphytes were the thoroughfare of squirrels and the mouse-faced woodpecker that flit from under tree to under tree. The sacred Logo tree stood guard over the forest at legendary intervals humming with all the supervisory deities long known chants of ancient rites. Birdsong and dirge for the dead days of our lives everywhere, life above and around, beneath, putrefaction, decay to nurture life and the tree. The trees would swoon now with a solemnity that was the signal of distress in their heavens high above our sorrow. It seemed they have been called upon by their very nature to share and hearken unto our inner sorrows swaying, in giddy waves in a melancholy jubilee in the heart of the forest and our souls.

We marched in a single file, our captors in excellent mood I knew not why. Now and then they exchanged a few words in their tongue. Their leader a man of stout build and yellow eyes was unusually quiet. He was apprehensive about what we knew not.

We on our part were still locked in the jaws of our customary silence, tormented by those terrorizing demons of our fate and destiny. We were marching according to the legend of Axum and

Nubia, the legionaires tramping across the passionate desert of our blood and land. The many uncountable dawns of our sojourn had ripped open the sunlit wounds afresh here in the coolness of the forest, our flayed flesh, the testing hide for drums long tuned by sorrow and tears. What would it matter now, our loves and hates in the raw flesh of time? We were walking in the day but were surrounded by an ineffable night of tree and leaf and an incandescent sorrow that thrust us into the rotting light of our despair. Our ranks had been reduced by death the ultimate voider of time and place, the lonely harvester of farms he had not planted. But we had wished, all of us, at all times had wished for his visitation and comradeship. But the reaper had heard the call of only a few ignoring us who needed him most befriending the innocent and the unaware. We could not even revive the parables of times long quashed in the blood knots of passion long dead in the reed valleys of the North. But our farewell to land and truth was still way ahead.

But now we danced, in our hearts, we danced with the infallible bird of the tall trees, the magical squirrels and the kingly lizards of his terrain. They focused our sorrow more sharply for us; our harried heart danced with the birds, squirrels and lizards of our dreams. They say terror is an instant companion who long known becomes an eternal ally, the sunset comrade in this desert. Does he not bestow some benediction through his acquaintanceship, his persistent will to be near in our hour of need? So we no longer fear him this offspring of the moonal eclipse and the equinoctial blaze, this daughter of truth and the manatees. The infallible bird flew in our wake propelled by our primordial smell, that elemental essence with which we would anesthetize the slave holds the dungeons the plantations and the masters' kitchen. It flew flapping its wings, wailing a long monody whoses strains I'd long heard and known. It came with us the last caravan burden beast of this desert. We grimly went on towards the lustreless territories of our doom. What virtues stir in his heart, this bird this grim companion of our sorrow? Where did they bestow on her the plumage, the colours of blazoning grief? She sent across the lower heavens a continuous monody, a long dirge, a passionate hymn that was both curse and benediction, we believed, on those who made us captives and ourselves. By early noon the bird flew away. She just departed abandoning our trail. She had come with us since the early morning alone. Perhaps we had angered her, perhaps we had not responded to her inner sympathy, her compassionate call to blood. She left us in the midst of a bamboo and palm grove on the edge of the forest. She left without warning just as it came bringing us a light hope of a reprive. So also had the silence of the forest that had accompanied us, companion to the monody of the infallible bird, a tremulous crab, carrier of our sorrow over the long trek. The silence, dressed in alligator colors, possessed the gait of the civet cat in his dance, the emphasis of our carrion days. It too rode along in the incandescence of the forest gloom and shafts of columnal light, announcing and echoing our crunching footfalls across the earth, the divinity that oversaw our days, maternal essence of invisibility, the only certainty we knew. Her divine sister was the echo among the trees, generated by footfalls on cracking twigs, crunching leaves, the singular cry of crickets, the wail of the bullfrog even at day, but above us the infallible bird, its wings flapping in our blood and sorrow, carrying and throwing back a thousand years (some say two thousand) of the invisible river. She punctuated our senses ridden by tragic demons, announcing for our captors victories reserved for the weak as they banquetted upon our entrails and drank of our blood. She was the sister of the invisible river. That much we knew for no one told us. The last trees fanged out like primal cobras spitting and hissing across the earth, gnarled step-children of the river and cousins of the infallible bird.

On the outskirts of the forest we hit the shores of the river, and the final stage of our journey.

ONE MORNING AFTER BREAKFAST, one of the prison officers came to call me away to an office. There I was told by a fat hairy man sitting behind a huge desk that I was free to go, that the case against me had been dropped. Six months of jail for a crime I never committed, and suddenly I was free to go. I sat completely unnerved and weary, more in pity for those who had inflicted this upon me than for myself. I had for these months searched my life, my childhood and growth in Virginia, my family, my father who by his death had released me from the crippling inhibitions of youth and that monstrous innocence that held my people in chain. I did not believe that there was a relentless retributive agent who was exacting payment from me for exactly no reason. I had no blemish on me except those imposed upon me by my historical sojourn here.

After almost two hours of signing papers which I was in no mind to understand, I walked out of the four iron gates to the road where the bus was to come for us. Soon it rolled up carrying mostly women and young girls, nubile betrothed lovers and tearful mothers of young inmates still awaiting trial. Yes, awaiting trial. Some of the guys I met inside were no older than I was, young dudes, largely form the alleys of Harlem and Brooklyn, mostly black or Puerto Rican. Some, you could see, had grown cynical and desperate. They had been here before. They knew they'd come back. We spoke freely about our fate, against our captors, those who sought us out for humiliation and suffering, those who could not hold forth any belief in our humanity, the law and its paid agents for whom we were only black statistics of crime, to be neatly collated and filed away. This was the pity and the sorrow of it all.

They were and still are kids in that jail whose lives are blighted because they are black and poor, and no one, no one will ever care about them. We were a community of young rebels, seething within, ready to come out to commit the crimes for which we had already been jailed. Our days were filled with dreariness, premonitions of doom and desperation. There was one little guy who sat in the corner everyday and simply cried. He must have been barely sixteen. His parents had just moved to Brooklyn where they had inherited a failing funeral parlor. This kid had been in the city only three months when he was picked up on a suspicion of rape. No one could raise his bail money of $20,000 dollars, and so here he was crying in a corner. But we were united by a curious sense of solidarity. Some refused to eat, some schemed to get food that their friends would not eat, some stole food, especially cookies and such stuff from underneath their friends' beds. When the lights go out, you would hear a quiet sniffing cry in a corner. A cry that would go on sometimes till the early hours of the morning.

I rode the bus to the main gate; I came down and walked through an army of people crowded into the waiting room, waiting their turn to visit their loved ones. There was quite a row going on when I arrived. A young girl with flashy eyes and flared nostrils was hurling thunderbolts at one of the guards behind the counter. He was a stout clean shaven black dude in the faded blue uniform of a prison guard. It seemed no one was paying the enraged girl any attention as she made intimate references to the anatomical features of the guard's mother, the decrepit state of his manhood, and the fact that he was a running dog and old ass-licking nigger for white folks who would soon be putting him to pasture, his active days of servility behind him. Soon a group of officers marched out from the inner offices behind the counter and led the girl away. The crowd, throughout this whole scene, was quiet, fidgety and patently bored. They were temporarily startled out of their lethargy when the girl was led away. For a brief moment, it looked as if they would rise up and attack their enemy, the hirelings of unfeeling laws, agents of terror and human degradation. But that brief quivering moment over, the waiting crowd slipped back into its lethargy and somnolent indifference. Whatever happened to that wild screaming girl (whose crime was her not knowing the last address of her imprisoned brother) no one can tell. She was led away by her captors screaming impotent obscenities. They, her people, had swung back into silence, the safest of companions, the badge of our endurance.

Outside, the world was calm. The city was covered in its eternal mist, a murky overhanging grey of outrageous exhalations from factory chimneys belching tar, smoke and black curly malediction. Right ahead was the landing fields of LaGuardia Airport separated from us by a narrow waterway and the smell of burning gasoline. Planes were landing at the front end of the field before our eyes, and taking off to the far right. The landers roamed in the left sky, then slowly, these monsters rode the air their wings heaving, vibrating in the still wind as they rallied for a glide close to earth, emitting loud booming deafening blasts, and soon landed, rushing now in fury across the field. Slow, they would turn round, majestic, glamorous, marvellous beasts slowly sweeping round, heaving now and holding the earth with a homing familiarity. Soon they would begin their glide towards the gates. The mystery was over. Those who were taking off on the far side would pause, heave on their butts, and like thieves in the night, take off on rushing wings and would soon be tearing through the mist, just going, going, far away.

Going away? Like thieves in the night! Escape! Go away. Where were those people on those planes going? Some for sure were only flying to other parts of Babylon, to the grey monotonous cities they had known since conception. Memphis, Los Angeles, Austin, Abilene, Chicago, Pittsburgh, Milwaukee. But are there any places of refuge, escape and of dream? Perhaps someday I'll go, but not to those places seared upon my memory, and upon the memory of my race. But where could I go? Where?

The bus soon rolled up and we were riding on the Grand Central Parkway towards the inner city. On the bus were a few released prisoners, those who had no folks to come for them and an assortment of people who had been visiting their loved ones, young and aged women clutching their pocketbooks, all tired and weary on this battlefield whose terrains they had known for centuries. There was one old woman sitting in front of me quietly weeping without a sound, mourning for perhaps a son locked away on that island. No one spoke on that bus that falling evening. The old woman blew her nose now and then, and sniffed like an abandoned dog in a crumbling corner. The silence on that bus was the familiar oppressive sister of sorrow.

I came down near our street. The neighborhood hadn't changed. The Texaco station was deserted as usual. The little delicatessen run by Mr. Rubikoff was open. I walked by, and when he saw me from hehind his counter he said "Hi Kid" as if he's seen me everyday these past six months. The kids were playing softball by the wall of the deserted warehouse waiting for the demolition squads and the developer's ball. The ball rolled over. I caught it and tossed it back to them. They went on playing, sweating profusely in the late fall heat, the young recruits for the slaughter house of racism in Babylon. But they didn't know, even though they sensed it in their tender green age. But it was there, what tugged at my heart-strings at eighteen coming out of jail for exactly no crime that I had committed. But my heart was not heavy this evening, this first day of freedom, because these younger brothers on the streets had purged the air and the land itself of the lingering pestilence of hate. So I could walk with a little cheer in my heart.

I was wondering what had happened to my friends. Did they know I'd been arrested? If they did, why didn't they come to visit me? I had given their names to the officers at the precinct. But I guess somehow they didn't know that I was in jail. The cheer in my heart made me dismiss all doubts about them. I was glad to be free, to be going to a place I called home, to two friends who were my buddies. I was praying that they should be home because I hadn't a key.

I climbed up to the apartment. The stairway hadn't changed. The same smell of assorted cooking from the rooms above. It was there in the long corridor, its antecedents long gone now, but kept alive and going by an assortment of offsprings that howl down here summer and winter.

I knocked on the door, first timidly, then louder. I waited. No response. I knocked again. And again. No one answered. I sat propped against the door for a time weary, tired, still smelling of the carbolic smell of the prison communal bath. I sat there, must have been for hours. I must have dozed away, fallen into a vague tremulous changing into a chain gang, and hearing the same never-ending dirge. Only in this dream; the familiar faces that always peopled it had grown dim, indistinct and blurred. But the profiles of those faces were the same, chiselled out on the tableau of this eternal dream; the apparitonal inhabitants retained their transmogrific personalities. But the familiar uncles, aunts, neighbors, the preacher, the community stalwarts and religious freaks, the boozy bar room perennials had not changed. The voices had not changed, the same low monotonous, yet now soothing spiritual, alternating with the jangling of chains as the gang clanged its stripped way in front of our porch, and descended into the valley and was soon gone, leaving behind only the sad monody sung in my father's voice that I have come to know so well.

The dream ended when I heard my name from afar coming over the hills and valleys of my weariness. I woke up. Standing before me was Mrs. Thomas of one of the apartments above. She was a kindly lady, solicitous about your welfare to the point of being annoying at times. But she cheered you up with her laughing greetings and incoherent stories of the day's news no matter which hour she met you. I always humored her and listened to her tales which would be about some forgotten event having to do with one or the other of her numerous children who carried on a long standing racket with balls, bats and shrieks whenever the spirit took them. Mrs. Thomas was standing before me in one of her faded dresses, the usual solicitation surrounding her, and in her eyes a forlorn look. She had been deserted by her second husband a few years back, abandoning her and the five children, one girl, the eldest who had left home at thirteen long before I came and whom Mrs. Thomas would have made me marry because I reminded her of her uncle in Red Spring, North Carolina. She lived on welfare and lost all sense of shame and anger as a result. In their place was a bubbling hold on life, a cheerful resignation, mildly tilted towards some vague hope that all would be well, soon, someday. Her children were her cross in Babylon, the lambs for whom she bled, wept and sang everyday in supplication to the good Lord above. The boys had taken to the streets, straying home now and then. When school was on they went, sporadically. The eldest was the apple of the mother's eye. Sometimes when Mrs. Thomas went away to visit friends in Newark for the weekend which was very regular during the previous Christmas season, the boy always performed marvellously, but at times took liberties with the younger ones whom he cuffed on the ears at the slightest provocation.

"They all gone, honey, where you been? They moved out, le me see, musta been around June when them two guys just pack up. Musta been like this time. Previous day they was making a helluva noise, crashing and cursin. Then they was shuffling the whole night. I wanted to come down, but didn't feel like poking my nose in, especially not with that colored boy who feels very superior. The Jew boy was always so nice, so gentle and respectful. The next morning they went. Haven't seen them since," she paused. She looked at me intensely, the same wearisome solicitation in her eyes.

When I heard Duke and Mel had gone, my heart went through a tumultuous rush and I was on the verge of panic. They would be somewhere just around the corner, waiting for me. There was something in Mrs. Thomas' eyes that told me that this was not true, that they were gone. Gone. My only friends in the city, gone. Turned and ran immediately after the cops picked me up and threw me into jail. My own friends.

Mrs. Thomas continued to tell me the story of their departure. Her voice droned on and on from a far away place. I was no longer listening. My mind began to wander over the events of the past year, since I left home. But I could not focus any particular piece of event other than the large ones that have stuck in my throat. The rest was despair and blankness. The voice of Mrs. Thomas returned:

"Honey, you got somewhere to go? You got folks here in the city?"

No. I had no folks here. I asked Mrs. Thomas whether she knew what they did with my stuff, my suitcase containing a couple of clothes and a few odds and ends. She didn't know. Perhaps the landlord would know, Mr. Slater who lived on

Berriman Street. Perhaps he would know . . .

The night was already upon the world when I set out to see Mr. Slater. It had come since I was lost in my reverie, and behind the barricade of memory and the shock of the departure of my friends. The kids had all gone. Mr. Rubikoff had since locked his store and gone to Far Rockaway. The Texaco station was deserted except for a moving silhouette of some forgotten attendant whom a gunman would cut down soon; all the previous attendants had been victims of armed robberies but the pessimism or cynicism of the station's management kept it open in the face of such persistent odds. Endurance and hope.

Mr. Slater opened his door. He was wearing a green bath robe in which there were a thousand birds flying over the heads of some moronic children playing in a New England meadow. There was a thick cigar, already half-smoked jutting out of his fat lips. He must have just finished his dinner. His gestures and voice were expansive and unusually accomodating. I had been delegated to see him once about the plumbing in the bathroom. He was on that day in a hell of a mood in which he came very close to doing physical violence on me. He had forgotten who I was. I could be a prospective tenant come to rent a piece of his real estate. Mr. Slater came from Barbados long ago when he was a lad.

"Hi kid, what's happening? Come on in, come on in," he bellowed between billows of cigar smoke. I walked into a large warehouse-sized living room containing perhaps all the gaudiest furniture on earth, some remnants of the depression era, some of indistinct and indeterminate ancestry, some the tawdry creation of some nightmare furniture ghouls for the expressed use of the vulgar rich. Mr. Slater waved me into a chair. The room had a strong smell of fried garlic and pork fat. On a cluttered table which was obviously Mr. Slater's work table, stood a large glass of a drink. I had interrupted an after dinner drink of our landlord. I told Mr. Slater my story. Slowly, his expansive accommodating mood gave way to a maturing anger which before I could finish exploded in my face.

"Those pals of yers was rogues, crooks. Those sons a bitches lef wit one mont rent, goddam it. They just up and lef one night taking even my keys and a mont rent owing. If I get my hands on those rats, I'll set the law pon them, son afabitch?

Did he know whether they had left my stuff in the room?

"What stuff? There was a battered ole suitcase with some stinking clothes. I have seized those till those goddam fellows bring me my one mont rent. Was those things yours, son?"

He said if I wanted them I'd have to pay the month's rent. Otherwise, he'll keep them and use them if my friends are apprehended (he actually used the word apprehended), to use those "lousy stinking ole clothes" as evidence of their fraudulence and guilt. Of course, I didn't have one hundred and five dollars. I had no money except a few miserable coins which could not even buy me a meal.

I thanked Mr. Slater and promised to bring him the money the next day in order to collect my clothes.

I walked out into the night again. Mr. Slater was wearing that quixotic look of a man who was sorry he had been angry and felt some sort of pity for his victim. He said not a word. He didn't acquire his real estate by remorse.

I walked down the streets, this time keenly aware that I must decide on something. Where could I go? Where?

At first I thought of returning to the building and asking Mrs. Thomas to let me stay the night. But I decided against that for no particular reason.

In jail I met a man who spoke about the faith of Islam. He was a clean shaven stocky dude who was doing time for armed robbery. He and a gang used to come around our section where probationers were held doing repair jobs, fixing lockers, sinks and stuff. He was about twenty-four, very dark.

There was a distant, almost saintly look in his eyes.

First time I met him was in the cafeteria. He was talking to three of the brothers, one of whom shared the same bunk with me. I sat with them and listened. Between short pauses, he carried on a long monologue.

"See brothers, the teachings of the honorable Elijah Mohammed are the only weapons with which we can fight against the white devil. He is the only man who can lead us to Allah, the true God of the African people. You folks got to ask yourselves where we come from. Yeah, where we come from? We black folks come from Africa. We were a race of princes, kings, royal men, running kingdoms built on gold. Yeah, gold. And diamond. That's why the whiteman came and preaching his Bible deceived us and took us away in chains to America. That was the beginning of our sorrow. We've been here four hundred years. That's how long. We were made to lose our dignity, our self-respect. We had forgotten the worship of Allah, the invincible, the Benevolent, the true God of all Black people.

I left the table out of annoyance at this dude. Here we were in jail and all he could tell us was some jived bullshit about some goddam god Allah who was supposed to be the god of black folks. Where was this dude Allah when we were caught chained and dragged here? He must have been busy doing something else. The more I listened to this moslem, the more angry I became. But I noticed that a couple of the young brothers were very keyed up, intensely listening to this bullshit.

A week later, I saw this guy at our table again. The attention on the face of the brothers told me perhaps I ought to go and listen some more. But I didn't want to. I wanted to go off somewhere. But we all had a routine as to where we sat for our meals, morning, noon and evening. So I went up, said "hi" and sat down. Brother Aboud was talking about Elijah

Mohammed.

"He was a simple man like you and me till Allah chose him to be his messenger. He was given the power to know what was in men's heart. He prepared himself to be a spiritual leader through fasting, prayer and keeping clean in the eyes of Allah. His message to the black man and woman was simple: Stop looking to the whiteman for your salvation because he ain't got it to give you. He ain't got it because he is lost, the condemned devil angel who still bears all the curses of the fallen one, in the way he behaves towards his fellow men, the way he is full of greed, deceit, cheating, the way he is mean, lying, cruel, the way he is gone around mankind war on all other people on the earth, taking their wealth, and reducing them to poverty and degradation. Elijah Mohammed the Messenger of Allah teaches that the black man can only save hisself when he separates from the white devil, leads a life of inner cleanliness, abjures the eating of pork the devil's own creature and follows the teachings of Allah on brotherhood self-help and love. Allah has a plan for all his children. Allah ... Praise be to his name ... Allah ... the Merciful ..."

This time I didn't walk away because I wanted to ask brother Aboud some questions. But the alarm had gone and we had to leave the cafeteria. That evening the brothers in my cell were talking about this dude, and about what the Moslems were trying to do for our people. One of them, Henry Sullivan, said he knew some brothers who belonged to a mosque in Harlem. That these were brothers who had been in trouble with the law and were now going straight and being Moslems and that kind of stuff. He said some folks used to make fun of the brothers and sisters because they wore long gowns (one guy said it was ladies dress) and the sisters went around in a stuff they call the veil covering their faces leaving only their eyes. They don't eat pork. Henry said he'd never been to the mosque but he heard stories of how the Moslems were taking in a lotta brothers who were conked out with drugs and didn't know what to do. They had a program to train the brothers in some stuff like mechanics. But he didn't know the details except that some folks in the neighborhood respected the Moslems, and others just, well, just made fun of them because they had too many rules and they dressed funny. But Henry said there was the Minister Malcolm who was head of the mosque in Harlem who was a serious dude. He'd done time, used to be a pusher in Harlem, had run quite a good number of rackets like women, dope and been in all major hustles in Harlem. Now, Henry said, this brother was a minister in the Nation of Islam and everyone said he was a helluva preacher. He himself hadn't heard this dude but he had a cousin who had attended all the religious sessions in the mosque.

I was not a religious guy. I told you I lost God way back at home in Virginia not because I didn't understand what it was all about, because I'd had too much of it, and didn't have time to even think about it. My mother was the center of our religious life; she was who shoved us to church and invited the preacher home to talk to us when we were said to be on the devil's road with disobedience, pride, and sheer infant foolishness. By the time I dropped out of school, I had dropped out of the church too. My father lay dying and I had to earn my upkeep and contribute to the running of the household. I hadn't thought about God since except when my father died, and they said he was going to heaven because he was a good man and that kind of stuff. And here was this dude now talking about a new religion and saying this was the true religion of black people. I spent nights turning over a lot of the stuff this dude was dishing; especially the stuff about how we were a race of kings, queens, princes and noblemen, and how slavery brought us here, how white folks enslaved us and brought us here to work on the plantations. Where was the god of the black people when they came to take the princes and the noblemen into slavery? I put it in my mind to ask brother Aboud when I saw him next. But I kind of dug the stuff about the white devil. It sure must be true, if you just pause and look at how white folks behave. They want everything—food, the best houses, the best jobs, the best clothes, the best booze, the best everything for themselves. Only themselves. When we ask for a little, we are told to keep our place, that we ought to be grateful for what we have. There ain't no jobs for us and when we go on welfare they say it's because we were lazy and shiftless. So we flounder here, lost in Babylon. Brother Aboud was right. There got to be a way to save ourselves.

The next Friday at lunch brother Aboud was there. He said that was the last time he was coming over to see us 'cause his time was up and he was getting paroled the following week. That kind of news made us sad because we were beginning to like this dude. We didn't understand everything he said, but he was the only grown up brother we met in jail who wasn't cursing and yelling like a mad beast. He was gentle. He spoke soft and he wasn't dreaming only; he could talk about salvation and black people and you won't miss anything like what he was saying was like the truth. It was like he knew what he was speaking about, especially when he spoke of dignity for the black man, how his salvation lay in splitting from the whiteman who's been the cause of all his sorrows since the beginning of time. Brother Aboud spoke to us of love; he said the word in the heart of Islam was love. That Elijah Mohammed the Messenger of Allah was the apostle of love; that with love we could break our chains and achieve salvation from the prison of the white devils.

On this his last day in our midst, brother Aboud was very quiet. He asked each one of us what we were going to do when we got out of the dungeons of oppression. We didn't even know when we were getting out. We were all silent for awhile, each looked into his secret and private hell of apprehensions and the collective purgatory of hope and all sort of possibilities. Brother Aboud looked closely at all of us, then he shook hands and said "Come to the mosque in Harlem, on the corner of Lenox and 138th Street. I'll be there. I may need y'all." Then he rose and left.

This was the beginning of the spring. He never returned to our section. We were certain he was out there in the mosque of Allah.

It was long after he was gone that I began to ponder his words, to miss the reassuring summer of a personality that broke through the bleak impenetrable winter of our despair and anguish. Maybe I didn't understand much of what he said, but I sensed a pair of wings unfurling in my soul, telling me that the bird of my youth was on the threshold of flight from its lonely cage. I remembered brother Aboud's eyes, benign, kind gentle eyes, something rare these days. Above all, he spoke quiet like, soft, even though the words were strong, words of liberation and of love. Like he wasn't angry in his eyes like most black youth are. But there was a fire burning in the deepest well of his being, released signal rays that announce upon the distant hills the coming days of our salvation. Salvation in his mouth and heart assumed mystical wings, well beyond the mere smashing of chains and the releasing of prisoners from long forgotten dungeons and torture chambers of racism and cruel history. It meant soon we should stand up and do things for ourselves; we would be free from the bondage of servitude to our base instincts, cleansed of the impurities of our association with the devil who had polluted our minds, bodies and souls. We would journey to the sacred homes of our real true selves, pure, elemental vessels for our African god who will restore us to our royal ancestry, wash and bathe us in his holy fire of eternal love and brotherhood.

I surfaced up on New Lots Avenue. I would take the train to Harlem and there seek out brother Aboud. He must be in the mosque. I would seek out this teacher who came briefly and vanished after having delivered his message of salvation while I was in the dungeon.

The number four going to Manhattan at nine P.M. that night was my chariot of love and anguish, bearing me to the first true home where my search and youth would be laid down. The car was half empty. Opposite me sat a couple. The guy, a black dude, was all dressed up in a mauve mod suit, a huge fuzzy magenta shoe, a large pendant around his neck, about five rings on his fingers. He wore a big afro and sported a well trimmed beard. His girl was also gorgeously attired, in a mauve low cut dress on which was glittering a thousand buttons. It looked like they were off to some do this Friday night. I kept my eyes on them until they left the train on Flatbush.

There was an old man in a corner very drunk who spoke to himself all the time. His eyes were half-closed. His clothes were unalterably filthy. He wore a light overcoat which had seen better days. It could have been light grey in its infancy but was now of an indeterminate color, further aggravated in shabbiness by what obviously was a community of long accumulated wine stains. His battered shoes were held together by a sturdy sole and a frontispiece of stout leather. He wore no socks. What he wore by way of lower and upper garments had obviously seen many years and little water. He kept on muttering something to himself. He would then, as if startled from some long forgotten nightmare, heave his torso up in an instant jerk. Then he would stare at the other riders, a blazing anger and contempt in his eyes, daring anyone to challenge him. Everyone turned his eyes away except me. He stared hard at me. I returned it with curiosity and sympathy if not an instant wave of eager identity, sharing and proclamation of solidarity with his misery. His glare slowly softened in response. Self-pity returned to his face, but he rejected that. He tried to restore his prefabricated anger and contempt. But the will had left him, for underneath he was only a lonely wandering wino, a sad old bum whose life was behind him, and for whom there was not a single ray of hope in Babylon. He was part of my own dark hammering sorrow.

The train sped on towards my salvation. A certain and sudden joy surged in my soul, as if I realized only then for the first time that I was free, released from the agony of physical and emotional torment of my loss of even the freedom to sleep in my own bed, the freedom to die by myself.

On ninety-sixth street, a well-dressed white gentleman got on the train. He exuded good breeding, condescension and arrogance disguised by a studied indifference to his rather unimpressive surroundings on this train. He strode towards the black old man who was now snoring in a soft alcoholic sleep. But the man halted in his track, reached for the overhead rails, swung round and staggered as the train began its journey again towards the crowded end to which most of the passengers had surreptitiously fled upon seeing the old wino. He managed to flop down in a small space right opposite me. All eyes were on him. He adjusted his overcoat, his elegant grey tie, bent down to remove a speck of ash from his bright brown shoes, tried to lean his right arm on the standing walking stick. When the last gesture failed, he lifted his head and was caught in the glare of eyes from all the other riders. He panicked for a brief moment, but got hold of his nerves, tossed his monumental nose in the air, fixed his blue eyes upon a Jack Daniels advert, and proceeded to ignore the eyes which he knew were still on him. He remained in this posture of elegant isolation, hauteur and indifference until I got off on

137 Street.

It must have been ten when I got down the train that night. The streets were still brightly lit. There were people everywhere, strolling night birds just walking the street on a balmy early fall night. The neons on the bars were bright. There was quite a bit of a crowd in front of Small's on 7th Avenue. A bar juke box on the corner of 138 was playing an old forgotten blues number. I was on Lenox and 138 now but there was no sign of a moslem mosque anywhere. I paused. I looked around for a while, taking in the indistinct personality of the neighbourhood. There was a bouncy, an almost carefree bravura in the lolling loiterers, a jauntily loose-limbed self-assuredness which was vaguely new and yet familiar. The music, the smell of cooking from the tenement houses, the rotting suggestive stench of garbage, all charged the air with an authenticity that I had sensed in many vague situations but not as strongly as this. For a moment I was seized by a haunting awareness of home coming. I sensed that my journey has at least for now terminated in this aroma of poverty and bright anonymity, and those on the streets in ridiculous hats and flamboyant garbs were my brothers and sisters from whom I'd never really been estranged. I was the prodigal come home. But I couldn't find the entrance to our house, my father's house, to the homestead from which I had wandered all my born days. No one could tell me, because I asked no one. I stood on the corner of Lenox, confronted by the promise of the feast of homecoming which turned out to be a piece of lenten supper without wine and celebrations and the fatted calf. I could not find the entrance to the home I had come to.

Then I saw a new group of comers. They were in long robes, long gowns of differing browns. The men wore nothing on their heads. The women wore longer gowns flowing to the ankle. On their faces were veils that covered their eyes. They were not in a procession but their progress down the street as they turned the corner into 138 Street assumed an eerie processional ceremoniousness as it wound its way and vanished through a gate two blocks down the street. Still they came down the Avenue, clutching their gowns, their eyes intently bent upon the road, silent, mute apparitions in the shadowy Harlem night. I stood there in utter fascination and excitement. These must be the moslems, those redeemed ones about whom brother Aboud spoke so fervently. They came from all corners. It was as if there were hundreds, no, thousands of them now, coming from all parts of Harlem from all over the ghettoes of Babylon, from lands of the deep south, the factories of Detroit, Pittsburgh, Milwaukee, Baltimore, Gary, Los Angeles, from the migrant camps of the northern farms of New Hampshire, New Jersey, from the crammed tenements of South side of Chicago, Watts, Cleveland, from all over Babylon, coming down Lenox Avenue, singing now in their infinite silence, singing Moslem hymns of nuptials, of wedding festivals, of turbaned princes on elegant horses, singing of the marriage feast and the savanna princesses, tall leggy long necked beauties with corals for teeth, attired in gorgeous robes of velvet, smelling of frankincense, cinnamon, of the fragrance of deserts, date palms, all of them African princes and princesses on the road to the ultimate festival of blackness.

Accompanying them were young riders on gaily caparisoned horses, their own horn blowers, adeptly handling the long leather flutes of Arabian nights, raising shouts and dust as they sped in swift gallops towards the black nirvana. There was a procession of young nubile maidens naked from the waist down, but veiled from the destructive power of the noon-day sun and the desert wind. On their feet were sandals shod in pure gold, their waists were weighted down with precious beads that with the tiny bells on the ankles, sent up into the howling flamboyant night air a music unheard before by human ears.

They were led by a stalwart horseman who performed daring feats on horseback with a scimitar and a long scythe-like pole of pure silver. He picked from the bowls on the heads of the girls the fruits of the feast: papayas, pineapples, large tangerines, mangoes the size of babies' heads, green coconuts decorated with jewels, long bananas on clustering branches borne in silver baskets. Beneath the horseman acrobat was a magician. He wore an enormous turban, held in place by a large ruby. He was in a leg gown topped by an elaborately woven tunic that revealed the matted hair on his glistening chest. In his left hand was a staff, in his right a decorated calabash. He maintained a beat which was not the beat of the procession; and whenever he tossed the staff into the heavens, he caught in its earthwards journey a dancing snake that wiggled around his huge neck and muscular arms. There was a smile on his face, a beaming smile of indescribable joy as he and the snake performed antics, leapt into the night air, illuminated by a thousand torches and the glittering lights of the eyes of those in the procession. The magician leapt into the air and sat upon a cloud of incense smoke, his snake, now a staff and his calabash a crown in readiness for the King who was not in sight but was sure to come someday to redeem us.

Slowly the procession receded, swallowed up by the night. The magician, the gifts and the horsemen were gone. The long gowned men were gone. The veiled women were gone. The avenue was empty.

I was alone. In a panic I rushed after the last departing member of the procession. I came close to him. I wanted to call him, to ask him to take me along to the festival. I got closer to him; he turned round without my calling him and asked "Brother, are you all right?"

I had fallen asleep sitting propped against the first tenement wall on the corner. Someone was bending over me, standing over me reeking of alcohol and sweat. He must have been 35, a young neglected beard on his face. He eyes were bloodshot. There was a wildness about them. But his voice was gentle, solicitous when he asked his question again:

"Brother, are you all right?"

I told him I was looking for the Nation of Islam mosque and for brother Aboud who was some kind of officer there. In a kindly voice he pointed to a door on 138 about two blocks away and said, "Sure I know brother Aboud, sure, the Moslems are holding prayers now and you'll find him in there."

I rose up slowly. This brother was still looking at me intensely. I realized for the first time that day that I was hungry. But that can wait while I looked for brother Aboud.

It was a little gate that opened when I touched it. It opened into a small courtyard completely empty. There was a hall on the right whose doors were opened into the courtyard. Here, gowned brothers and sisters of the procession and my dream were seated. A man, tall light-skinned wearing a short beard was standing in front of them. As I approached the hall, one of the brothers walked towards me with outstretched arms of welcome. It was brother Aboud.

OUR CARAVAN, PERHAPS THE LAST REAL CARAVAN *of the desert now entered a wide greenery, a large expanse, orchards planted by no one, blooming with a yellowing tree filling the air with a magnificent smell that satiated our hunger. It also made us infinitely lighter on our feet. We had left behind the sands, gravels and the soft moss-covered leaf carpeted grounds of grief now. The smell of the river was in our nostrils. The long stretch of grassland extended where the eyes could not see, on the horizon the elemental plants standing guard. The grass, loose limbed, tall, roamed on the edges of the orchards.*

Half the morning after and we had hit the river. A great sense of joy surged through us, as if our journey was over. We knew that this voyaging river was winding homewards. Homewards? But there was an abiding quietude. The threshold, vertical upright in the exploding sun, the light on the river, deep revelatory beams telling of all the caravans and the abyss. It was the river that would bear us away.

A calmness had descended upon us, after the instant surging joy proceeding out of arriving home, given now by the insanity of the poisonous sun, companion of the biting gnats and the annoying flies of the water. By early noon, we had been put into a long boat ferried by stalwarts from that country, our face set towards the downward flow of the river.

We rode silently locked in that glow of homecoming across a wide expanse, reeds and marches on the banks, mangroves, black water sentries bent water-sippers. The hour was born anew, the river was the terminus of our previous lives. Our journey now lay on the river, the path and the patterns of our lives. The bird had abandoned us to the river. Our inconsolable heart shall set sail. It was more than chance bringing the voyager home. Those calamitous dreams peopled by allergic cats pawing our hearts, in the rising waters, the roses of creation, the terrestrial waters, deeper still deeper. On the shores beside the burning lilies were the doves, divine birds that lived in the mystical palaces, guardians and messengers of our inner calm now.

We were rowed for three days and three nights down this river. The banks changed in rapid succession from mangroves to hills that stirred the abysmal depth, giant custodians of the sacrificial blood that flowed beneath them. So river by river we drifted on, speeding down towards our ultimate destiny. Once this river, invisible, was now the passageway of our passion. The sun shone across the river before and behind us, forever.

Then one day we came to the sea that was to take us away. The unchained river, incarnated in the embrace of the sun, had at last led us to the ocean.

On the third day our boat set sail.

I FIRST MET HIM IN A BAR at Osu. The Red Rose to be exact. I had been hanging around waiting for some of the boys to show up. I had already gone through a couple of beers, and was still incredibly sober, judging that my stomach was empty. Then he walked in. He was with a large headed Ghanaian fellow whom I knew vaguely as having lived in America for years attending universities. The American was a tall fellow with a large bushy head. He walked with that slow slouch that always distinguished a black American. They took a table close by and were soon intensely engulfed in some conversation. I heard bits of it. It was political. It's always political with chaps like these. The Ghanaian was trying hard to sound like his American Negro friend. Their voices matched, so I couldn't really tell who spoke when.

My own thoughts were on other matters. I was without a job. Let me introduce myself. My name is . . . forget it, it's not important. I am a product of the new Africa, a university graduate, and some sort of a writer, actor, broadcaster,and a tragic hero. I'll explain all these in the course of this narration. I lost my job because the new government had fired me together with 500 others predominantly from my ethnic group which had not voted for the new rulers at the only polls we've had this decade. Long Live Democracy! The reason why I was dismissed I believe was that I was appointed to my job by the previous government, I mean the civilian one under Nkrumah, the man who was driven out by the soldiers. I was accused of being a collaborator with some acts of corruption that went on in those days. So after a series of decrees and eloquent proclamations, we went civilian. That's another story. I mean how we went civilian, what great acts were performed by the shining apostles of democracy.

But I must return to my story and stop going off on tangents, as the English say. So I lost my job. I received a cyclostyled letter signed by the secretary to the cabinet that I must not come to work next Monday. And I had put in seven years in the National Institute of Cultural Revival where I served faithfully one of our illustrious chiefs who received a D. Phil from Sussex and liked to boast about how Africans spoke Latin as far back as 1482. After collecting a lot of money from some foreign bodies, he vanished into Borneo and Papua where he was supposed to have come upon some startling archaeological and anthropological evidences about how the languages of Papua contain words to be found in Ga (one of our languages) and how the way in which their women carry their babies was extremely similar to ours. Then he went off to south of India to discover the same evidences. We are still waiting for the publication of these startling revelations. But I am straying off again, damn it. What was I saying? Yes I was fired this morning. My boss I hear wasn't fired because he has a few friends in the government—before and now—and I had taken part in all kinds of corruption. But let me get on with my story. The next time I digress, throw away this book, then go and take a drink of orange juice. You will like that.

I was saying, I sat down listening to the conversation of these two fellows. The American had just apparently rediscovered the Americo-Ghanaian. They had met back in the States. They shared some common friends who were also strong nationalists and African revolutionaries. I sat there listening to this Ghano-American unfolding some weird political ideas of his. The name of Fanon came up once in a while. Fanon was a Martiniquan who wrote the book called *The Wretched of the Earth* in which he built some fantastic theories of revolutionary action based on the great earth-shaking Algerian revolution. In this book he condemned the deadening influence of tribal culture, (which he saw as part of a feudalist order) attacked the national bourgeoisie, (they deserve every abuse, the clots) and proceeded to call for blood, blood, blood. He died of a blood disorder in a hospital in Baltimore, Maryland, USA. He also wrote a book in which he attacked all black people who hung around white people (they deserve it, the parasites). He himself married a lily white French woman.

So these two fellows were talking about Fanon. The Ghano-American guy I had met once at some cultural evening at the Egyptian Embassy. He had with him a quiet Arab girl. He was introduced as a journalist who was attached to the national newspaper.

I was sitting there listening to these two fellows as they solved all the problems of Africa that night. Especially the novelist chap. Everything that everyone had done since he left for America was bad, the people were evil for wanting to make their lives a little better, the leaders were crooks, everyone was a thief BECAUSE THEY HAD NOT READ FANON. I am not a very political person, but I get excited by rallies and marches. I used to go to the West End Arena in the late forties to listen to the leaders and to some pretty wild speeches. The Party was very strong in those days. At University I joined the student wing of the Party. Kwame Nkrumah came over himself and launched the youth wing. We were so excited to see him, our leader. Later on they said he ruined the country, so they deposed him, of course. But back to my story. I was sitting still waiting for my friends but the rogues were taking so much time to arrive. So I heard this fantastic conversation about African politics and Fanon (didn't someone write something about his ribs?)

But let me tell you a little bit about myself, because then you will understand exactly what happened in this bar on this fateful day in August 1970.

I was born in a small village. My father left school very early because his father would not look after him anymore. So my father went home to his mother's village and there became a fisherman. Later on, he was apprenticed as a tailor. When he finished his apprenticeship, he made a few clothes and gave up. He made my clothes, large and roomy, into which I was supposed to grow. Whenever they wore off, he didn't believe it that clothes made of khaki could really become torn. My father was a disciplinarian, a man who loved his wives and children but didn't spare the rod in order to spoil us. There was very little food or anything around. But I grew up somehow, believing I was destined for something. I believed in mysteries. I still do. If you were born close to an ancestral shrine, your uncles played brekete drums every night, and whenever you came home on vacation you were taken to pay homage to all the old folks in the shrine, you will grow up believing in mysteries. Don't misunderstand me, I am also a modern, very modern African.

I went to the University of Ghana where I was taught by an assortment of English-men who produced a number of first class holders whose training in English verse and prosody was unsurpassed. Some of them were back from long post graduate studies abroad with impressive chains of degrees hanging down their breeches, carrying on stalwartly the eminent traditions of their teachers. I had a great time at the University though. I read all the quaint books at the instigation of the only two human members of the English Department. Our university is a fine institution. It is run by a group of very well meaning Africans with active support from their English friends. We believe very strongly that a university is a place where a group of men and women live in the name of truth. Our university lives for truth. Nothing disturbs our university—changes in government, military coups, earthquakes (only sometimes, it's on a fissure line) and famine. Our scholars do not write books, but this is not important because who ever heard of university scholars writing books? Our students are meek, humble, brought up to obey the rules and regulations; only once in a while, moved by some devilish spirit, they go into town to throw stones and shout obscenities. But I said we had a great time there. The Lido was Lido then. The girls used to come over the walls, with the agility that surpassed a professional acrobat's. We had fun.

Then I started writing poems. No, no, no. I was writing them long ago in my elementary school. I was writing this poetry which was made up of imitation of Alfred Lord Tennyson. Can you believe that? Tennyson. I wrote a book of poems when I was fifteen, together with a classmate of mine. We published a book hand printed. My friend could write beautifully and we called the book, The Forster Tennyson Poems. I was Forster, my friend was Tennyson. But let me jump. I took up writing poems at the university again. My teachers really liked it, and even awarded me a prize. My poetry was based on snatches of songs I remembered from childhood. It was all crisp and clear, and I drew a lot of attention because I was a poet. But more about that someday.

I was jerked out of my reverie and the journey to my childhood by a set of familiar voices. My friends have arrived. You must meet them. This one is Sammy. He drinks like a well. At one time he was a good accountant, but he lost his job some years ago through sheer carelessness. He set up his own business managing the accounts of a number of stores owned by Lebanese and Syrians, when he is sober. This other one is K.K. We simply call him K.K. even though these are not his initials. He is a little fellow weighed down by an enormous head that tapers from a broadly massive base into a cone. He wears glasses, so his eyes look very funny behind them. But he is a very smart fellow. He manages his own drugstore. Then there is Boba. Boba is also my friend. He comes from my hometown. His problems are food and sleep. He can eat food laid out for twelve people, true. And, listen to this; immediately after he finishes eating, his eyes begin to swim; he will fall asleep in exactly five minutes. We used to play a great game of just timing him. And lo and behold, we have never been proven wrong. Then there's Ahmed. He always comes last, in everything. He never buys drinks on the simple premise that he is a Moslem even though you will never catch him dead near a mosque. He never once refused a drink for as long as I knew him. The mystery is that he never gets drunk. They all come in, my very close friends. Oh, then there is Ava. Ava is a superb cabinetmaker; he hasn't been to school like us; he provides a kind of silent scheming leadership that steers us to where women and fun are. I forgot to tell you. We are all unhappily married. Everyday we meet, someone will have a horrendous story about how badly his wife was treating him. How he was not a happy man at home. But we all knew these stories were fabrications, designed to make us feel easy when we go women chasing.

So there they were: Sammy, K.K., Boba, Ahmed and Ava, my best friends in this hour of need. I ordered some more beer and pulled closer some more chairs. Just as the drinks were being opened, I felt I was being watched. I always know when strange eyes fall upon me. My forehead begins to burn and my head tells me to look up. I did instantly. The two chaps I told you about were both looking at me. The American Negro was staring in a vague uncurious sort of way, while the African journalist was intensely on the verge of saying something. I wasn't too sure whether he remembered our last meeting. I think he did, for a moment later he was walking toward us. When he got very close, I rose up to meet him.

"Remember me?" he asked. Now that's the kind of question I find always difficult to understand. Why? What does it mean to walk up to a fellow and ask him, "Remember me?" What kind of question is that? When I am in a rude mood, I always want to answer no and tell the fellow to go to hell. Why should I remember this pompous ass who really thought (I secretly heard) he was better than everybody because he's been educated in some fancy American private school and in an Ivy League university? (Someone told me later that he went to Brown. It didn't make any impression on me for the simple reason that I didn't know what in god's name it was).

"Yes," I said. He paused right behind Ahmed who I knew hated anyone standing right behind him. He said it took your soul away. I suppose this was one of his Moslem beliefs. Ahmed was about to tell this writer fellow to stay away from his back when I noticed that a sudden change had come over him; he looked faintly disturbed and worried. Even though I don't like him (I suppose you will say I was jealous of his fame as a journalist. Perhaps I was, so what?), I felt a quick beat in my heart. Now that look I was familiar with; it's when a fellow is on the verge of asking a favour or something like that.

"Can my friend and I join you?" Now that is something that I really detest, imposing yourself on people just like that. I saw K.K. rearing to make one of his obscene remarks to the man; so, because I think that K.K. is a cheeky bastard, I winked to Boba to shut him up. K.K. fears Boba, see, because when Boba is hungry, he laughs at him, so Boba threatens him with physical violence which he never carries out for the simple reason that he is too lazy to make the effort. But now and then he would nudge K.K. with his elbow to his side and that always hurt K.K. who, as I said, is a skinny little fellow in glasses. So K.K. shut up.

"Yes, of course," I said. The Brown man hesitated for a brief while as if he wasn't too sure. But this time I couldn't guess what was going on in his mind. None of my friends were very happy that I had agreed for these two fellows to join us. So what? I invited them; it was me who lost my job, wasn't it? So I said once more to make it abundantly clear, I said:

"Yes, of course, feel free," in my best English accent (someone once said I had an Oxford accent though I'd never been there) and added "Certainly." You should know, of course, that there are several ways of saying this word "certainly" in English. Anyway, I said "certainly" in a high dive intonation contour which implies a whole set of emphasis, warmth, culture, affection, concerns (deep) and just a tiny little bit of apprehension. See what I mean?

The two men came over, carrying their glasses and their chairs. We had made room for them. They sat down, placing their glasses right in front of them and bashfully, as if on cue, taking a sip, setting it down before them, right at the very spot where they had first put them. There was absolute silence in the bar. Business wasn't very good, so the Ibo owner Mr. Ben hadn't started playing his gramophone, which when he played it, you could hear the music at Mataheko. (We were in Osu, the other side of town). There was complete silence. Our two new friends were obviously very embarrassed by this silence, not knowing what to do. We were also apparently embarrassed because we don't really know these fellows. But hell, this is Africa where people are free, uninhibited, happy and unworried. I read that somewhere. A single housefly obviously an escaped prisoner from Ben's fat wife's kitchen adjoining the bar, flew straight and landed on the American's glass. Now, believe it, when I say houseflies are the weirdest creatures in the world. They will fly straight into your mouth in the middle of a sentence and you can clear your throat a thousand times, you can't get them out. They are really weird.

Take this one now. It chose to land on the rim of this perfect stranger's glass. Then it gleefully rubbed its two front legs together and after staring at the man for a split second proceeded to march down the glass towards the beer—there was just a mouthful. It proceeded slowly, now it would pause, then it would pick-up again; then it would pause. It kept on doing this for a long time; then I suppose it actually misjudged the nearness of the beer, and before we could blink, this fly had gone and fallen in the American's beer. What do you with a fly in your beer? I suppose the answer really depends on who you are, where you were born, your cultural background, your conception of the world, belief, or disbelief in God, gods, Allah or deities, your sense of mythic structures, or your personal hygiene. Someone has to spend a fellowship year at Oxford researching and writing a brilliant paper on the subject. It will expand the frontiers of human knowledge beyond belief.

Anyway, the fly fell in the beer. At first, like all stupid clots who fall into things, it panicked. It tossed its legs about in a vain effort to swim or at least get out of its predicament. But houseflies were not made to swim. The more it struggled, the more it got wet with beer. There was complete silence. The fly fought with all its strength. It got hold of all the straws in the beer but in vain. Then it began to uproot first the giant trees, the bushes, the shrubs as it grasped for breath. Then it bellowed, it raised a mighty sound that rent the housefly heavens with a loud shattering effect. As its booming voice was heard by the housefly birds of the air, they fled frantically seeking to perch on those giant housefly trees that were no more. Then it began to crawl to the bank with its last strength. It ate the housefly sands on the shore in its deep agony. And with its last breath, it raised a shout that shattered the housefly moons, skies and sun. Then it died.

Did I tell you I was a poet? Now you know. The fact of the matter was that the housefly was drowned in the beer. By its death it raised a new problem. When it fell in the beer, it was a problem; now, in death, the housefly was the source of a big, big problem. Well. How many people have ever been caught in a similar situation with a drowned housefly in their beer? Pretty tricky, if you ask me. Your reactions, as I said before, are determined by a number of unconscious cultural factors dealing with religion, god, man, the environment and the wider issues of the hereafter. That's it, the hereafter has actually got a fat lot to do with a dead fly in a beer glass, my friends.

By this time, the fly's death had exhausted all of us. As if we had been released from its hypnotic death fight, we all came to life at once. The American Negro (he later said I shouldn't call him "Negro" which made sense because strictly speaking I was also a Negro but somehow I didn't ever think of it) stretched a long arm to grab the glass. He was reaching inside it to remove the dead fly. Ahmed was swearing in Hausa about flies in the night, Boba was reflecting upon his empty stomach, Ava began to stammer some instruction to Mr. Ben's little boy who was manning the store (we once cheated him, with Ava's help, out of a lot of money over some good White Horse Whisky). The Brown man was preparing an elegant sentence in his head. The American grabbed the glass and tossed the beer out of doors into the yard. The table had come back to life. The journalist spoke,

"Well, let me introduce my friend brother . . . "

He mentioned a number of names. The only one I remembered was Lumumba.

"Oh, is he from the Congo? I mean Zaire, they now call it Zaire, sorry," I asked, once more making my voice as cultured as possible.

"No, no he's from the States, man, the States." We really liked that, the way he said it, "from the States, man, the States." That was really nice. We really liked American slang, it's really nice.

So, since it was my party, because it was me who lost a job, I introduced my friends to the two gentlemen. The American from the States, man, had a firm hard handshake. The Brown man had a limp shake which was neither Ghanaian nor American. Anyway they shook hands with us all round.

"Can we call you Mr. Lumumba then?" I asked the man from the States. He said "Yeah." We like the way he said it. Soon four new sweating bottles of beer arrived on the orders of Ava who was now obviously very agitated because we were no longer going to speak our native language. Only English. When situations like this develop, Ava always becomes very nervous and angry. Long after, he would even accuse us of complicity in a plot to speak English in order to show him up. He's like a university lecturer friend of mine who when you introduce him insists on your prefacing his name with Doctor, otherwise he would think you are deliberately undermining his standing in the community. But Ava's is really not a serious problem because he was not bothered with status or anything like that. He only simply felt left out. In fact, we used to play games on him. Once there was an Englishman who loved hanging around us everywhere we went sitting at goat feasts. Someone had gone and goaded Ava into speaking English with him. No. Ava does know how to speak English. But he speaks only pidgin, not the proper one with Oxford accent, and grammar like some of us who studied it. Having been dared sufficiently and with enough gin in him to float a medium-sized canoe, he went over to the man and said with a straight face, "What is my name?" Of course, the man didn't know what the hell Ava was talking about. Meanwhile the plotters had burst into a deafening guffaw. Ava was really angry that day. I'd never seen him so angry in all my days.

Boba simply loved everything about the United States. He's never been there and he'll never probably go, but he loved the

American or Yankee way. Being somehow older than all of us, he saw the GIs who used to be at the base at Takoradi. He loved their way of dressing, their life-style, the way they walked, talked, bullied, spent money and all. He loved everything about them. There's no cowboy film that has ever come to our city's cinemas which Boba hadn't seen. It meant going without supper in order to stay awake to see the film. A man loving food as much as Boba does who forgoes the passion of a dinner for a cowboy film must be congratulated on his tenacity and sheer capacity for endurance. Immediately the film was over normally around 10 P.M. Boba would drive home at top speed where a gigantic dinner was awaiting him. In fact, Boba is the only man I know who will rise up in the morning prepare breakfast, then go back to bed, lie flat on his back, put the breakfast tray on his stomach and proceed to eat breakfast in bed because he saw it in an American movie. So Boba asked brother Lumumba to tell him about the States. Boba was very excited because he was sitting by a real live American. He later told us that the man wasn't speaking proper slang, because he was only a Negro. I told him maybe.

Brother Lumumba spoke in a deep soft voice. His eyes were greyish brown, like a cat's. His face was long. He wore a luxuriant beard which was linked with his well trimmed moustache. As he spoke, he lay two large brown hands upon the table in front of him as if he didn't know what to do with them, as if they didn't belong to him. His eyes focused on nothing in his lean long face. As he spoke, they became slowly agitated, animated by some long ago passion, as if his memory was struggling over a terrible event somewhere there in the depths of his being. He said he was from Virginia, at least that was where his folks came from. He grew up in a small town; it wasn't important to tell us the name. He quit school when he was sixteen or so and after his father died the following year, he left with a couple of friends for New York City.

Boba's eyes lit like an oil lamp when he heard those words "New York City."

The man continued his story:

"Well, I did a little time for something I didn't do. After I got out of jail, I joined the Moslems." It looked as if he didn't like to talk very much about his Moslem period. Ahmed, our Moslem expert showed a big surprise, didn't know what to say. Brother Lumumba said he was there when brother Malcolm was assassinated on February 21, 1965 in the Audubon Ballroom in Harlem. He was one of those who split from the original Nation of Islam to go with brother Malcolm and his Organization of African-American Unity. He and this brother Aboud who took him into the movement. Before the split he had been one of brother Malcolm's personal bodyguards, a member of the Fruit of Islam. They'd gone to Chicago or Phoenix together to see the honorable Elijah Mohammed, the Messenger of Allah. Malcolm loved him like he would love his own brother. After his famous trips to Africa following the split, Malcolm used to speak about Africa as the true home of all black people, the land of our ancestors which was rising up again. He spoke of how Africans looked like us, how we in America had been "brainwashed by centuries of slavery and the feeling of inferiority," he said, his eyes now dim and distant.

Brother Lumumba was really moved by what he was saying. I just stared at him wondering what exactly was going on. Boba had lost interest. Hunger must have wrestled with his burning interest in America and won. Ahmed was quite interested. K.K., the arch cynic, was patently irritated by all this. The Brown African journalist was keenly looking at his friend, showing not only an infinite understanding of what was being said, but also a deep sympathy and identification with the man's story. Ava lost interest in the whole proceedings for the simple reason that he did not understand what was being said.

Brother Lumumba went on. He said when brother Malcolm returned from Africa he spoke of the true religion of the world being Islam, with its emphasis on brotherhood, and love. He spoke of how he came to understand then that the only evil white man in the world was the American white man who had taken his forebear from Africa, kept him in chains for centuries, worked him as a beast of burden till he died. Brother Malcolm, he said, spoke of the coming struggle for freedom, the need for the readiness to die.

I was getting tired of all this sad talk, all this business of readiness to die. Here I was, having been dismissed from my job because I was a friend of Nkrumah's after seven years of making some (I don't say much) contribution to my country. A young believing idealist lad who saw the birth of my nation, who really worked for those ideas of a united people with one aim, one country, one destiny. Sacked for what? So I came here to celebrate. I mean to mourn (see how I misuse the English language at times; it is not my native tongue, I kept telling them) and here is this Lumumba fellow talking about dying. If he wants to die let him go with his Fanon disciple to Algeria or somewhere and die. Why is he telling us? I was getting more and more angry. Where did he get the name Lumumba from anyway? He is not even a Congolese. I was truly beginning to be angry with this chap for spoiling our evening. We were just going to drown my sorrow in beer and then pick up some girls and go to the Star Hotel later. This fellow was ruining it all. I turned round to look at Boba. He had fallen asleep with his head on the back of the chair, his mouth ajar. Boba was asleep in the middle of the whole stuff about dying. K.K.'s glasses were misty, not from tears but from late evening fatigue. He would start wiping them very soon. If he starts, he never stops. You have to signal to him that it was all right and that he could wear it. K.K. is always neat. When his glasses get misty, you must know that K.K. is slowly and painfully dying of boredom. Ava was silent and unconcerned. Ahmed was vaguely interested, being something of a romantic person. He loves stories of death and valour. He was, however, the greatest coward in our group. In fact, his wife beats him regularly. You'd see Ahmed sometimes, his lips smashed into a pulp, when you ask him, he'll answer with a disarming truthfulness and the sorrow of a bruised ego that it was his wife Amina Baby who beat him. Amina Baby is an enormous woman from Lamakara. Her name is only Amina, but when Ahmed is drunk once in a while, he carries on this persistent chant in which Amina Baby are the only words. So we naturally took to calling her Amina Baby. She is much older than Ahmed, that's why she beats him. They have a gorgeous daughter who will be the talk of the town fifteen years from now, I bet.

I didn't say anything against brother Lumumba's monologue. He continued, transported now to a far away place, the story of his life. He began to speak again, in a slow voice which was almost a whisper.

"I was one of the brothers who was supposed to guard him. We were there when they gunned him down. Three guys just got up and started firing at the man who was our Leader. Do you know, we who were supposed to guard him ducked and lay sprawled among the chairs?"

His voice was hardly audible now. His face was now a mask of intense lines and inordinate sorrow.

"We were there when they killed our prince," he whispered.

I was suddenly seized by a sense of remorse for being just now irritated with this chap. There was something he was saying which distantly touched the deep recesses of my being.

"But," he soon started again, this time as if he had returned from a visit to the memory of that tragedy which still haunts him, "but he gave us a vision of ourselves, of our true homeland Africa before he died. He showed us the way to the East where all good things spring from, the fountain of our manhood."

The man had started his thing about Africa again. My irritation came back. I wanted to tell him to shut up for a change. I remembered that I'd lost my job and my anger rose up like a cobra ready to strike. I took a look at his face and I was sorry for him again. There was something deeply disturbing lodged in his soul.

Boba was now awake. Hunger had now reduced him to a state of lethargy. He had lost interest completely. He had decided in a small corner of his mind to get drunk. We always had to keep a check on Boba when he is drinking. He carried in his large bulky frame and sheepish eyes a deep-seated violence whose eruption we had seen many times. There was the night for example when Boba, just a week after his mother's death, had come to the Red Rose a subdued and almost absent-minded creature. He drank compulsively. We couldn't restrain him because we knew how much Boba loved his mother. So we drank very seriously together. The night was black when we stepped out to find our bleary ways home to our neglected wives (the parasitical bitches!). Boba was going to give us a lift in his Peugeot 404, a second-hand job he bought from a pock-marked Ada smuggler. As we got closer to the car, we noticed someone almost lying on the bonnet. Boba went up very gently, he went up to the person and asked the man what he was doing on his bonnet. The man jerked his head up, took a mean look at Boba, turned round and said something very very rude about Boba's mother. Now we all knew that Boba's mother had died just this past week, and here was this fellow referring in very uncomplimentary terms to her anatomy and personal hygiene. No. This was not fair. This was down right cruel. A deep sorrow rushed over Boba; his mighty frame trembled like the whale washed ashore on a beach, surrounded by the children of the nearest fishing village. It occurred to me that this fellow didn't know Boba's mother was dead. How was he to know? Abusing people's mothers wasn't anything strange in our part of the world. But it was hard for us to tell Boba not to tremble. K.K., his glasses shinning over his eyes in the dark night was already anticipating a fight. He always loved a good fight so long as he was not involved. Sammy stood behind us pissing in the gutter and belching loudly, saying, "Boba, kill him, kill the beast."

That night was a terrible night. We left the fellow bleeding through the nose and mouth, lying still behind the exact spot where Sammy had pissed.

Boba ordered more beer. The journalist fellow from Brown was very very quiet, his mountainous forehead glistening at its many bulges, his eyes sad and yellow (this seemed to be the natural color of his eyes, I was to note later). Throughout the long disclosure by his friend, he had been very quiet, even though it was obvious that he was agreeing with and sharing the emotions of his friend's sad and terrible tale.

So we continued to drink. And the man, brother Lumumba spoke about Africa the homeland, the spiritual birthplace of all black folk. He actually said it like the, "spiritual birthplace of all black folk." Very moving indeed. Very moving. He talked of how brother Malcolm used to sit down with the brothers after the regular Friday prayers and talk about the struggle of the black people in America, Brazil, Cuba, the Caribbean, Canada, Central America, and how that struggle was linked with the struggle of Africans. "The problem of the black man anywhere is the problem of the black man everywhere," he said.

"So I began my education after brother Malcolm went from us. I read all the books I could lay my hands on. I quit school when I was sixteen. I didn't have much chance to read and get an education. Brother Malcolm used to say, if you want to know what hell you are in, go and read the books about your folks, read the history of the slave trade, and the suffering of centuries we went through from the first day our forefathers landed in America till today. So I read. I studied the writings of the great African leaders—Lumumba, Nkrumah, Nyerere, Sekou Toure . . . " K.K. started giggling because the man's pronunciation of these names was terrible. I nudged K.K. in the side to keep him quiet. One of his most obnoxious habits, K.K. I mean, was this uncontrollable urge to laugh just when people are dead serious. K.K. will come into a room where fellows are having a very, very serious conversation. He will stand there and if everyone ignores him and went on with their discussion, K.K. will sniff the air and without any warning, say in his squeaky voice: "Some one has flatulated in this room. Can't you hear it?" I once told him that you don't hear flatulence, except the noise. He answered that that was exactly what he meant—with the worst kind, you actually hear the smell as it assails your nose. K.K. was like that. Once he was chased for almost a mile by a Moslem fellow at prayer whose stick K.K. lifted for the heck of it. But brother Lumumba didn't even pause. He didn't even notice.

"I joined a group of black activists whose goals included the unification of all black people, reparation from the white man for all the years of labour he had forced from our race, and socialist revolutionary action that will destroy the bastions of capitalism. We all studied Fanon's *The Wretched of the Earth:* it became our Bible . . . " This time I almost laughed. But I didn't. I knew that the Brown chap was looking at me, and since I didn't want him to go writing about me and my poetry, I kept quiet. Well, it was also because I was beginning to like the American, this brother Lumumba. "We studied Che Guevara, and Fanon. Above all, we learned of the example of Patrice Lumumba. It was soon after that I threw away my slave name and recovered the names of my people. There was just about twelve of us at first. We used to meet in the apartment of this other brother from Tunisia, Ibn el Rafiq; he was a cool-headed dude who knew all the books. He said he had even once worked with Brother Ben Bella and had shaken hands with Che himself. Our studies were important for us. We were concentrating on the question of our own national bourgeoisie as outlined in his book by brother Fanon, analyzing the relationship between oppression and the national bourgeoisie in its alliance with exploitative capital, forming a formidable point . . . " Boba let off a callosal fart. I know Boba well, he must have been trying to suppress the bloody thing for hours, and after having failed to make it noiseless, succeeded in creating the loudest noise of a fart I've ever heard. He himself looked very startled and rather surprised. Boba is a man who respects himself, and to be caught unaware by an unplanned fart among strangers including an American Negro was tantamount to loss of dignity in a very significant way. What were we to do? We are not like Europeans who go around farting indiscriminately and are never even slightly worried about it. To us a fart in public is a serious matter. Men have been known to have hanged themselves because a fart had dropped off them before their mothers-in-law.

Talking about mothers-in-law reminds me of Sammy's mother-in-law, an enormous woman of independent means. She had gone through four husbands comfortably without any visible signs of wear and tear. She was then enjoying the first glow of menopause, teasingly beautiful, as fat as a porpoise, but with a fantastically beautiful face. This was the period she chose to torment all the husbands of her three married daughters. For three months, she would move into one of her daughter's homes and spend the time reminding her of what an impressive pedigree she belonged to, how she could have done better for herself, and how she couldn't sleep at night because of an infernal noise that came from their bedroom. (This is an oblique reference to the son-in-law's snoring). She carried on this crusade of torment for about one year. On the next round, she moved into Sammy's home to stay with her daughter Bertha. Sammy and Bertha had no children, so you could imagine the kinds of innuendos that flew around—bleak references to men who were not men, etc. Sammy, as was his custom, ignored her with an alcoholic dignity, you know, the kind that walks proudly off but nearly falls down with the fifth footstep. The old fat virago felt cheated, for what was the use of tormenting someone who didn't show the slightest sign of hurt? So her programme of harassment intensified. She plotted and schemed and finally hit on a plan.

But here I go again digressing shamelessly from what I was saying. Suffice it to say that Boba let off a fart and conversation was cut short. Brother Lumumba, a quixotic smile on his face, realized that he was again a member of the farting smelly human family, and it was the same everywhere; a plagued tormented hungry, under-fed, joyous, melancholic, sad sad humanity for whom each moment was enough, for whom there are dreams, not the dreams of others, their own dreams, however paltry, not the dreams of political ideologues and plain bores who will condemn them because they saw food and wanted to eat it, who will preach at them because they had visions of cargoes bringing clothes, bread and sustenance for their aching bodies. Whose corruption it is if these who preach the high minded moral garbage are themselves thieves, fornicators, acceptors of ill-determined largesses and tormentors of women. So what?

We drank our beer and the night grew, and as Sammy pretentiously announced in ordering another set of beer, the night was still young, very, very young.

Mr. Ben had come back sometime earlier. The Red Rose was filling up, for, this was Friday night. The gramophone was going. James Brown was screaming "Say it Loud, I'm Black and Proud!" The Red Rose had the loudest gramophone in town. While the music goes, you actually hear the music. The loudspeakers were always faulty so the music acquired a grainy sandy gruff tone which just made it jump. Red Rose was the home of James Brown whose music had swept the west coast of Africa before it. It was music to dance to, it had beat, rhythm, the thump thump of stamping feet hitting the earth, aggressive, sensual, sexual. I can go on using all the cliches, but suffice it to say that James Brown is good.

The girls were beginning to arrive, the Friday night good time girls, secretaries who are hardly literate, typists who can't type, air-hostesses with enormous behinds and smelly mouths, ministries girls with hanging breasts, bank girls with crooked legs, gorgeous madonnas of the tropical night, great beauties with hair stinking to high heaven. But can they dance, these women! They are as sophisticated as angels. Watch them as they walk across the dance floor, just walking, not dancing, and you see the glide of primordial animals flying and sliding across the empty earth at time's beginning. Quite good that last description. I told you I was a poet.

Brother Lumumba was very animated now, downing his beer with that bravura which I have seen among stealers of booze. His grey eyes were ablaze like those of a civet cat's as he enveloped us with his deep and moving sense of solidarity and brotherhood. We were, it seemed to me, the kinsmen he had lost; this homecoming had been a dream he once had, he said, and now he was glad to be among his own.

Boba had slipped into his customary lethargy preceding inebriation. K.K. had polished his glasses over and over. Ahmed had lost interest in our table and was staring at the girls, a lascivious gleam in his beady eyes. Sammy, elegantly in control of his drunken soul was with us, keenly following the monologue by brother Lumumba. Ava had left for the urinal from where it didn't seem as if he would return soon.

Our Harvard African novelist, once the brother was no longer talking about revolution and Fanon, had lost interest. He showed signs of irritation about this whole conversation about brotherhood, independence, Nkrumah and whatnot. These were nothing, nothing, compared to Fanon and revolution and the theory of mystification. Ghana under Nkrumah was nothing but excrement, corruption and thieving. It was nothing. But the American brother was his friend; they had met long ago in the States when they went to a party on Morningside Heights where a large corps of the Nationalist boys had their base—a few African students from South Africa (who are the aristocrats of all Africans because they come from a great urban culture), a couple of chaps from Kenya, two Arabs who had suddenly upon arrival in America discovered that they were Africans, one Ethiopian who was rumoured to be closely related to his imperial majesty but now hates all monarchies (he looks forward to the succession in order to declare Ethiopia a people's republic and proclaim revolutionary freedom, whatever that is). He was a sad little fellow who said very little.

The brother from Ghana was introduced to this group. Talk was about Fanon the whole night, and from that day forward he had found his savior. If he spoke three sentences, one was bound to be a quotation from Fanon. After this rich private school, he went on to Brown (where else could he go, not to Livingstone College, Georgia?), but he took his revolution seriously. So he became friends with the liberals, left-wing revolutionaries and even the near anarchists who saw in him the true combatant of the coming struggle in Africa. He himself was set ablaze by the call of revolutionary blood. He wanted to go to Cuba and march with Castro, Cienfuegos, Guevara, Raul and the boys coming down the hills bearded and in tattered clothes descending upon Havana, in a triumphant sweep to the music of machine guns, rifle fire and mortars set off in salutation from anchored ships. But when he really felt he wanted to be there, Castro had already taken Havana, the blockade was on, and Cuba had really begun a revolution. But he had had enough of capitalist America; he hated all those longfaced Yankees whose money he had been living on all those years. He hated their promiscuous women who were eager to shower on him a great deal of sympathy if not love. He detested capitalism and its attendant materialist philosphy. In short, he had become a burning revolutionary. Where indeed was a revolution seeking combatants, asking for men like him to come and spill their blood for the fatherland (any fatherland)? Where indeed? After searching beyond the closed shores of revolutionary Cuba (god dam Castro for not knowing his true comrades), he discovered Algeria. Holy Moses! Why did he never think of it? Hadn't the revolutionary genius of Fanon the prophet of the black nirvana himself been born in the holy fires of the Algerian struggle? Isn't *The Wretched of the Earth* a treatise that came out of this sacred struggle which, Marx be praised (and Lenin and Mao but not Castro), was still going on? So he packed a travelling bag and with a girl companion he set out to die for Algeria. The girl was white, of course. That's the virtue of the black revolution. Its true spirit proclaims its hope through the thighs of white women whom they end up hating because they hate themselves so much. But she was so human, tender and possessed of a sharp analytical mind that tore to pieces any marvelous treatise on capital formation and the scientific nature of imperialism without reference to Marx or Engles. And she had very strong views, which, if the spirit took her, she could express with such power and vigour that warmed the revolutionary cockles of her companions's heart. So off they went to the wars, ta ram, ta ram ta ram. Algeria watch out, your salvation was at hand. On one blazing Sunday they arrived. The revolution was over! The fellow went raving mad. He was brought back to the States where he spent some time in Bellevue recovering from nervous exhaustion and mental fatigue. The bloody Arabs, without letting him know, had called a halt to the war and were actually at Evian negotiating with the French. Never never trust an Arab. Just when you expect them to make a revolution, they abandon it and start talks.

This was the beginning of his decline, nay his loss of confidence in Africa, Africans, Nkrumah, and his motherland. After a while he came home, and with the help of friends got a job at the national newspaper, the Globe as a feature writer. They couldn't use anything he wrote because no one understood them. His supporters said it was because he is actually a genius. Aren't they supposed to go mad at one time or the other? Aren't they supposed to hate everybody and everything? Aren't they supposed to write things which no one would understand? Everybody and everything at this newspaper was wrong. The Editor was a clot, a sycophantic nincompoop who didn't understand him. Above all, Kwame Nkrumah and everybody connected with the government was a corrupt, evil-minded moron. So in the end our friend dropped out and went to live with an Algerian research student, a sad-eyed sallow girl, who exuded so much gentleness and compassion that it was sad to look into her eyes and feel how much she felt for him.

To cut a long story short, our friend went back to America the beautiful, the only country which he really knew and loved. All that I am saying, I heard long after this night when he was sitting with his friend brother Lumumba at our table at the Red Rose on this night when I, because I belonged to a certain tribe, and because I did a job under Nkrumah had to be sacked!

Brother Lumumba was an amazing man. How he could talk non-stop astounded me. Slowly I began to develop some respect for him, a deep abiding respect. Half the time I didn't understand his slang which got more and more blurred as he proceeded. But I made a vague sense of what he was saying. He communicated his deep love for us, his long lost brothers, for the fact that we Africans were so simple, uncomplicated. He spoke of how they in America were "fucked up," those were his very words. When I asked the journalist what was the meaning of "fucked up," he said it was American slang for confused. As he was the one who said it, I believed him. But why didn't brother Lumumba use "confused" which was a simpler word? These Americans and their English!

The Red Rose resident band made up of some boys who used to hang around the bus stop at Anumle Village, arrived at about 10:30. The night was still young as Sammy had said. After spending about half an hour tuning their instruments, they struck up their signature tune, Take the A Train. After playing that for one minute—during which the sax player was obviously still tuning his instrument—they sat down and started grinning at us like a set of fools. Someone said these boys smoke a lot of wee, the Indian hemp, which can send you to the asylum if your head is not very strong.

The leader of the band was the son of a well-known washman who used to wash clothes around Achimota when we were there as students. He used to hang around our school compound, after running errands for his father, a dirty wet-nosed urchin who will throw stones at the slightest provocation. There he was now in a twinkling jacket, a knee-length boot, a pair of skin-tight trousers, and twanging a guitar. I must say he looked quite presentable standing there beneath the blue lights. He played the guitar like a demon. Then there was his drummer, a fellow with a head that looked like three pieces of rocks lumped together. He had two large startled eyes, a nose that was just a pair of man-holes, and two small mousy ears. What can you expect, I mean musically, from this man? But when he touched the drums with his sticks, the most near perfect syncopation rhythm and jam jazz and beat came out and you will be hopping on your leaden feet till thy kingdom come. God doesn't deny a man everything; if he didn't give you good looks, don't worry. Search hard; there is something he'd given you and you better find it fast. The bass guitarist was not an interesting looking chap; in fact he looked uncomfortably like me—large ears, long nose, a long jaw, an enormous head, funny woozy hair, and two eyes widely set apart. And black. Jet black, In fact, a couple of times fellows will stop me in the street and ask whether we were playing that night. I always simply said yes just to avoid trouble. People are so stupid that if I had said it wasn't me they would have gone into a long long palaver about what, who and whatnot. I don't like arguments over silly things like that. So I just say yes and the matter ends. But when he is playing and I am there everybody says "your brother plays well" and all that. He is not my brother. Then there was the vocalist; a small fellow who always wore jackets one size bigger than himself. He was a very animated fellow, and quick to action. I once saw him handle a drunken woman who fell on him as he sang Blue Moon with such superb artistry that I took an instant liking to him. He just lifted this woman up by her large buttocks and shoved her onto the dance floor in a rhythmic fashion, so that the woman continued to dance lying down, just carrying on the rhythmic motions of the push.

So. We were sitting down, drinking our beer, and listening to brother Lumumba giving us the story of his life. The band was playing a Congolese dance tune; people were dancing; conversation was good and I had even forgotten about the fact that I had lost my job. Well, I actually hadn't forgotten; I was only vaguely aware that it was real. Why not? I am among my friends and the world wasn't really a bad place after all. Who cares?

A group of Europeans walked in accompanied by African girls. There were four of them, the engineering bush-dwelling type you find here who have hung on after the empire was over in the belief that they were serving Africa—hard faced, hard drinking sons of bitches whom Africa has really destroyed. Three of them were holding onto three beautiful, nubile, innocent African girls. I instinctively knew that these were school girls whose stupid parents were either corrupt or unaware of their teenage daughters' life style.

Accompanying them was a familiar and ubiquitous Englishman called Thomas Rollston. Rollston came to the Gold Coast to serve as a colonial officer. He rose through the service and became the Director of Recruitment and Training. A couple of his old colleagues rose with him. One was called David Mackintosh who was Director of Scholarship. Another was Robert Pitchfork who stammered like a gas light. He was the Director of Public Works. But these last two had gone now. Wait a minute. Mackintosh came back to advise the revolutionary government of Ankrah and Harlley on scholarship matters. But Thommy Rollston stayed on after independence. It was known that, like all of his colleagues, he hated the nationalists, especially Nkrumah, with a passion. Yet somehow or other he convinced the new rulers to keep him on because he actually possessed over twenty-five years of experience which he persuaded them to use. So independence saw Rollston, the arch colonial servant, still at his post saying "sir" to these black bastards whose guts he hated. He stayed on as director and when Africanization came he moved up to the cozy position of advisor—a lot of money and no real responsibility. Of course, he wasn't the only Englishman they kept. There was another called Cecil Allen who was a good lawyer and readily became a power to reckon with in this black and proudly independent nation. Rollston was, as the story went, unable to live in England anymore. That's what Africa does to you; she gets into your soul. Rollston came in this night into the Red Rose with these three engineer-looking Europeans (they looked German or Swedish) who were accompanied by these three school girls. Rollston and his group as usual were followed by a young light-skinned boy whom I once met at a party. He served as a regular errand boy.

Anyway. They walked into the Red Rose as if they owned the place. You must see how Mr. Ben who had been half-asleep the whole evening long jumped up and began to salute and grin and shout salutations at the same time. He was obviously overjoyed that these important beings had come into his humble night club. The Europeans greeted him with a hearty condescension. Meanwhile Mr. Ben's little boy brought a clean table, a plastic table cloth, and a set of fresh glasses elegantly poised on a tray. There was an awkward moment when the group was poised between apprehension and embarrassment; the men, because here they were with school girls who were young enough to be their daughters, Rollston because his light-skinned African friend was too eager to be seen as part of the entourage; the girls for the simple reason that they should be in their beds or doing some home-work at this very hour. They were all apprehensive of what the others were saying. They were the focus of all eyes, but not out of hostility, but rather of curiosity and on the part of the older professional girls, undisguised envy or jealously that these infants were taking the white bread from their mouths. Didn't they say that out of the mouths of babes shall he ordain strength? The preacher was right.

As if on signal, conversation dried up at our table. Brother Lumumba who was the centre of our evening had stopped talking. An overwhelming sadness descended upon him. He watched in a strange way the new group sit barely four feet from us. In fact, we could hear their conversation. Brother Lumumba was transformed. That distant look I said was in his eyes when he spoke of the death of Malcolm returned, but this time with a deep impenetrable sorrow. His eyes gathered mist as he turned them away from the group and focused them upon us as if we had the answer to the hidden mysteries of his soul. He put his chin in his palm, then went into a reverie that lasted for over five minutes.

Meanwhile Boba had woken from a recent sleep, and in lieu of going home to eat, he ordered the bar's tsitsinga, a kind of kebab with a lot of hot pepper, really good with beer if your stomach is strong enough to take it. He ordered as much as eighty cedis worth, which means about twenty tsitsingas. But we were not alarmed because he surely will devour all of it. K.K. was polishing his glasses once more. Sammy was complaining about how beer makes one always want to go to the gent's. Ahmed was now looking at the young girls with the Europeans with more intensity. Ava hadn't come back.

The next table had ordered a bottle of Martel Cognac with ice and ginger ale. Rollston had sprawled in a chair nearest to me reeking of some ghastly eau de cologne and cigar. One of the three Europeans, the youngest one, was telling some story which was obviously very funny because the girls were all giggling like idiots. The centre one, belonging to the tough hardened and the oldest of the Europeans, was a beautiful girl. Her eyes were a steady pool on which there was a water lily each not yet in flower. She had a nose that was short and abusively curled like a little cat in the tight centre right beneath those eyes. And her lips were, well, very inviting. Her neck was long, covered with lovely rings. She sat with her neck carelessly but deliberately tossed to her left side as if she was cocking her ears towards a whisper that was not there. Then she smiled. She ruined it all by smiling. Her upper lip curled in that brief smile into a hideous fold like the fold of the roaming snail. So I turned my eyes away.

The second girl was darker than the other two; she had a largish forehead, dome-like and hanging over her eyes which were not exactly small, but overshadowed by the pendant miracle of a forehead. Her face was broad, like an open field in which a sudden mound is erected which was her nose, stout yet distinguished because there was something benign about it. Her mouth was well cut, if a trifle poised to insult at the slightest provocation.

The third girl was light, one of those light girls whose parents would chase a black boy away with a machete. She was tall and willowy. Her look was almost moronic; perhaps she was retarded, but she wasn't because she was the most talkative of the three girls. She laughed loudest, flashed her teeth across the room—she had one bad front one—and sounded more experienced, more knowledgeable about the affairs of this world.

Mr. Rollston was talking now. He was a very large man. He moved around as if he was cast in a barrel from his chest downwards. He had a square face—red—with two piggish eyes that never showed any light. He had spent about thirty years in the country, retired now on his colonial pension. He loved being here in this country; nothing can send him back to England where he might not even have a living relative. Rollston's young friend was sitting on the edge of his chair very eager to get drunk. He had already downed his first glass of brandy and ginger. Mr. Rollston really didn't like this boy following him around but on nights like this he needed him. He serves as bodyguard and (they say) later as something else. He was a tall thin red-skinned boy of indeterminate parentage who had dropped out of school and now works for Mr. Rollston. I will not go into the whole sordid matter because it turns my stomach. He was good looking, almost pretty the way girls are. I wonder, now that I think of it, where he came from. But it's no matter now because he is dead. Memory!

Memory! I remember that night well now, as if a cinema screen was unfurled before my eyes and everything started afresh, all over.

The journalist who has been very quiet most of the evening leans over and whispers something in the ears of brother Lumumba who has been for a long time gone on a long mental journey. His eyes register some sensibility at last acknowledging what his friend has said. But he is still angry about something. There is not so much as anger but a deep unsurmountable and indiscernible hatred on his face now, ready, tender, ready to explode the oppressive universe into a thousand pieces. The band is now playing a Nigerian high life in the style of I.K. Dairo with a couple of conga drums imitating the dondo without achieving the same blended effect of the dialogue of original instruments. The music is however soothing. One of the Europeans gets up to dance with the tall light-skinned girl. But brother Lumumba is watching them with a kind of intensity which I've never seen in any human eyes. He turns and whispers something to the novelist who looks momentarily alarmed. But he quickly overcomes this, and with a quixotic smile on his lips, he nods his head. Boba is snoring again. K.K. is wiping his glasses. Sammy is humming a tune completely out of touch with the music of the band. I suspect he is trying to sing the song being played. The result is sheer disaster. But no one can tell Sammy that he is a poor singer. Ahmed has turned one hundred and eighty degrees from where he is to look at the dancers, especially the girls.

Slowly, brother Lumumba gets up. He slouches rather than walks towards the other table. He says something into the ears of the beautiful girl, the one who ruins her face whenever she smiles. She actually blushes, looks at her escort who is definitely not interested. So she gets up and follows brother Lumumba to the dance floor. About a split second later, the Brown

African journalist also gets up and goes through the same motion, slouch and walk and whispers in hanging forehead's ears. She doesn't blush because she is too dark to. She looks questioningly at the elder European who shrugs his shoulders. They too walk off to the dance floor.

The drums have taken over now. This is the time when dancers talk with the drummers, their companions and the music. Brother Lumumba dances as if he has danced this all his life. The Brown chap dances as if his waist is broken and his torso crushed by the burdens of revolutionary ideals. But they dance. The girls, obviously teenagers now that they are on their feet, move with the grace of gazelles, jauntily tossing their behinds in the air at an angle which will gladden the heart of an artist. Their breasts, from the flimsy upper garments they are wearing, jump erect into the air, their hands lingering in front of them, probing the atmosphere and the space between them and these strangers; their eyes now alive glowing glistening almost liquid with magic and celebration at this hour. This is what they came here for; to dance, to become one with the air and the space with the mystical blend of the music of drums, rhythm, and the mystery of being itself.

The dance is long. The partners begin to sweat. Brother Lumumba is erect but possessed of a grace which hides the volcanic outbursts of his rhythmic sense. In this dance it is clear he is home. This is what he too came here for. The writer chap is doing his best, but the man has been ruined by some desperate malady of the spirit. Not that he cannot dance. But his soul is dead, dead because his humanity is dead, killed during the ordeal of his sojourn. He has not come home yet. He will never come home. Those two girls simply soar in the air now, descend on wings upon the earth, their grace, power and magic like the outpourings of the racing demons of all passions, all being.

Very soon the dance is over. I am watching the faces of the

Europeans. They look quite happy and seem to be enjoying themselves immensely. Mr. Rollston is desultorily drumming his fingers on the table. His young friend is looking at us as if he wants to hurl some insult because K.K. is now staring at him.

The journalist and brother Lumumba lead the girls back to their table. The tall light-skinned one, the one I said looked and acted experienced, is in a towering rage, walking back with her partner.

"How dare you speak to me like that, how dare you?" The two Europeans get up to enable her squeeze through to her chair. The girl still hangs on to brother Lumumba; now she is screaming obscenities in Twi. The two Europeans walk towards brother Lumumba whose earlier anger has returned blazing now like the light of a thousand forest fires. He starts to speak to the men and I cannot understand what he is saying because his slang is so fast now. I can only catch a few flying words. Rollston is up on his feet saying something about bloody Americans who come to Africa behaving like bloody clots; the Europeans are swearing in English, German and some other language. Rollston's young African friend has also risen on his feet and is addressing both us and brother Lumumba. The journalist stands in the background swaying I believe. The girls are all speaking at the same time. There are a million voices. The Europeans and Mr. Rollston's boy walk towards brother Lumumba. He is facing them with his right side towards us screaming in slang. Soon, soon I notice the flick knife open blade steady, glinting in his palm, held in a steady professional untrembling manner by a man who obviously knows how to use it. They crowd him and the knife flashes. I see its flash about a thousand times as it cuts through the masses of bodies. He stands over them just slashing, slashing away. Then the screen was snapped back and everything went back in time.

Mr. Rollston's friend was lying prone across the table. The glasses had been upturned in the melee. The drinks had been spilled upon the floor. Blood was all over the place. The voices had all died. Mr. Rollston was holding his left shoulder, badly cut, a gush of blood pouring onto his fat stomach. He looked deathly more from sheer fright than from any mortal wound. The three Europeans had all sustained cuts on their wrists, arms and bodies. The younger one had his left cheek almost carved off down to his jaw. The girls were screaming in all the languages of the land. Boba, dead dead Boba who was so far from the fight because he had been sitting in the far corner of the yard was shouting, "I've been cut, my mother I've been cut, my mother, I've been cut." K.K., Ahmed and Sammy were on their feet. I was on my feet. Ava appeared from nowhere screaming. I looked around. Our journalist friend was not there. He had probably fainted from seeing so much blood. Later on I learnt that he simply took to his heels.

I am telling all these now at such a leisurely pace that my readers will think the whole thing took such a long time happening. No. I have no proper sense of time, measuring time by any mechanical means destroys the depth and autonomy that time, real time, in all its mystery and magic, imposes on all things. Time is events, time is place immeasurable, beyond recall. Time is the record of the mythic dimension of our interaction with our surrounding beyond the direct acts, beyond the immediate recordable now. Time is the truth which is shattered ungathered and frozen forever. I told you I was a poet, didn't I?

Brother Lumumba was still standing over his victims, his knife in his hand and on the verge of moving in on his enemies and annihilating them once and for all. I don't know where I got the strength from. But I saw his long sinewy right arm raised in the air in deadly aim at Rollston who was in a state of half comatose in his chair. Somehow I knew I must reach for that arm. Not that I cared two hoots about Rollston, but that I cared about this man, this demon from far away. Cries were already going up over Mr. Rollston's boy. They were saying in the Ga language that he was dead. I got hold of brother Lumumba's raised arm. He swung around and aimed the knife at me. But in a split second he saw my face. He must have seen also the history of his sojourn and our common voyage in my eyes. He understood. There was no time to lose. We must leave, run at once, just run and keep on running.

K.K, Boba who has since quieted down when he realized he wasn't hurt, Sammy, Ahmed and Ava were standing right behind me. As if on a gun starter, we began to cut through the crowd. My hand was in brother Lumumba's; the knife was in my pocket. We tore through the crowd that was now paralyzed with fear. It parted into two for us. We waded through it surrounded by a wall of absolute silence, fear sitting like a pall upon this group of recently happy dancers. Boba was lumbering behind. I called to him and he almost knocked K.K. down in his elephantine rush.

We made for the gate and the streets, the murmuring voices behind us now, locked into the heaviness of the night. And the night swallowed us up.

We plunged into the night, not exactly aware where our flight led. Brother Lumumba still clung to my right arm. My steps were firm as I knew every corner, alley and path in Osu. A surging murmur from the Red Rose reached us but we were far away now, fleeing towards where I knew not. Boba, Ahmed and Sammy had fallen back; it was only Ava who came close upon our heels, panting. Soon I heard him scream to the others, "Me-me-meet us-ur at the-the-the junction. Bo-bo-ba, me-me-me-meet us at-at-at the jun-jun-junction." Brother Lumumba and I just sped on across the hedges, gutters and soon we were crossing the main street. A few loiterers paused in their tracks obviously frightened by our flight. We sped past them like demons, and vaulted a gulley near the Regal Cinema. We skirted a small dunghill. We were soon in a grassy field, dotted by the coconut trees. It was then I realized that we were fleeing towards the beach.

The shore here was dotted by steep alcoves where we used to camp while swimming. I had not anticipated how close we were to the edge of these falling heights. Before I knew it, we were rolling, falling down, just falling. Finally, we landed deep beneath, right at the edge of the water, still firmly holding onto each other. We were covered everywhere with wet sand. We lay panting, breathless, exhausted. It was as if we had been transported within a short brief moment across distances and time itself. We must have lain panting in the sand for what could have been hours. I was free from brother Lumumba's hard grip now. He was crouched on the sand some yards away, curled up like a little boy who is afraid. Then I felt the water washing against me, gently, soothing. Then I heard the voice of the sea, soft sibilant balmy, as the water caressed me, sending its spray into my face. I lay still. The sea spoke in a low voice now, a deep howl now, and a gentle quiet whispery tone now. It was as if we had been paralyzed by the magic tones of its voice. It was as if we had been in this place for always.

Suddenly I came back from the soothing hold of the water. I rushed over to my companion and shook him hard. "Get up," I said, "we must be on our way; we must go." He rose up as if he was waking up from a long peaceful sleep. He wiped his face with his hands and stared hard at me.

"Where to?," he asked.

I looked at him, understanding momentarily that there was no time for words of explanation.

"Just follow me," I said.

I led the way, instinctively eastwards. He followed. We ran close to the water's edge. The night was deep. But the sea had lit the shore, bathed it in a strange luminous light, grey, unreal but clear enough for us to see our way as we ran. We must have run for about a mile when I remembered Ava's instructions to Boba. What junction did he mean? We ran on, however, I leading the way and my companion close on my heels. We were filled with an indescribable strength. Our pace was regular. Then I remembered. Why didn't I think about it?

On the great coastal road that travellers had initiated many years ago with their feet, there are many stop points where little markets had grown. These were like oases in the vast desert of the coastal plains where the travellers weary with fatigue stopped in order to eat, drink water, relieve themselves, and rest for a while before they proceeded on their journey. There are seven of these resting places that go back in time. Today, even though the pathway had given way to a motor road, these resting places have not disappeared. Instead, they have grown as junctions, central points that now link sometimes three or four roads. The markets have been superseded now by the important roads. Little towns have grown up on these spots that still retain their character as oases, rest and meeting places, and points of departure for all travellers.

The nearest of these was about five miles due north, on the roads that cross southwards and eastward. When Ava said "at the junction," he was referring to this particular spot because on lazy bored Sunday afternoons, this point served as a rendezvous for us. Here we would gather at noon to drink palm wine and eat a special type of tsitsinga made of the grass cutter's meat. There was an old woman and her husband who sold palm wine and tsitsinga under a little palm leaves shed a few yards from the road. Sometimes a greying old man whom everybody called Papa Soja would come in with an ailing guitar and play for calabashfuls of palm wine from the wayfarers. He was a very jolly rascally old man with all his front teeth missing who was in the Burma Campaign as a magazine carrier. He had the disconcerting habit of sticking his tongue out through the upper part of his mouth and in a grimace sing an obscene song he said they used to sing on the march. This was the junction.

We continued to run. The sea-spray was now in our eyes and we couldn't see for the mist and haze. But the light from the ocean was on for us to find our way. I turned round to see how my companion was doing. He had fallen a little behind. He was only a dark limping silhouette now against the long sweep on the shoreline punctuated by coconut trees, falling alcoves, and far back in the distance the old Castle. I called to him. He responded in a loud voice that he was coming. I saw him bend down momentarily. Soon he was up and running towards where I stood. I turned round and continued. My companion was close behind me now. We fell into a regular pace.

After we had been running for some time, we came to a point where the alcoves had given way to a wide low-lying sandy beach. There were clusters of coconut trees huddled together here and there like a group of conspirators in secret council. I decided that we should move into the sandy tracks. For over a mile we ran across this beach, the sea now about twenty yards away, its magic distant now, made up of changing voices from low moaning whispers to loud deep growls that accompanied the crashing of the waves upon the shore.

Soon I saw a ghostly huddle of white forms way ahead. At first it looked as if it was stationary. As we drew nearer, I noticed that some of it was detached, some of it was even moving. I paused suddenly in my track. My companion came right upon me. He halted. He and I scanned the night trying to fathom the creature or creatures before us, now only a few hundreds of yards away between two coconut groves. I asked my companion to wait there. He sat in the sand panting.

I went down on my hands and knees. I crawled slowly towards the creature or creatures. I came very close to them. It was a group of apostolic worshippers, a Christian sect that held its prayer meetings on the beach dead at night. I came much closer. They were seated in a circle. In the centre was their leader carrying a long staff, I turned round and crawled away.

We cut back right behind them and hit the grassland on the edge of the sand. My companion kept close to me. We still had some distance to cover before arriving at the junction. The night was still deep. But our eyes had become attuned to the darkness, our feet familiar with the earth. My companion had lost his shoes earlier on sometime in our escape. He didn't seem even to be aware of it.

We ran through the grass, the rising breeze of the sea behind us. The night noises of insects were everywhere. There was the persistent cry of a village of crickets that seemed to be everywhere. Bullfrogs were wailing, the echoes of their cries heard across the vastness of the grassland. Once I stumbled and fell, my right foot caught by a grass root. I fell flat on my face. My companion lifted me up by the neck.

We were now running parallel to the sea, towards the east. Very soon we had to change directions, move northwards in order to make for the junction. We passed by a village on our left. Some dogs sent up a desperate howl into the air.

From underneath the coconut groves we soon arrived at the junction. It was in a state of deathly silence. We paused to catch our breath in order not to wake the people. We approached the junction very slowly and carefully. The market was empty. A few stray goats and sheep were roaming it. The spirits were busy with their wares. We skirted the market swiftly. Then it occurred to me that the place was where the palm wine shed was. I rushed towards the shed, my companion close behind me. Standing in front of it were Boba and

Ava.

Boba was very calm and collected. Ava was speaking, but I hardly could understand what he was saying. Ava is a stammerer, and whenever he becomes very agitated, you can hardly hear anything he says. You heard only a series of stutters that go twt twt ttt twt. And that would be it. We didn't have time to begin to sort out Ava's words. Up on the road was parked Boba's Peugeot 404. He signaled us as we came closer to go away. He was pointing to the car. I turned round, my companion following. The key was in the ignition. I got into the driver's seat, I motioned my friend to sit down. Boba and Ava were walking towards us as I moved the car into first gear and moved. Boba and Ava had paused. There was a sad, an almost melancholy look on their faces as we left them. They vanished when we turned the first corner on the road that leads towards the north, our safest route of escape now.

We swung onto the new road that had been built a few years back leading to the Dam. It was linked with an old road that cuts across the river towards the north. We drove in complete silence. My companion was slumped in the passenger seat next to me. He was very still. His eyes were half closed.

Strangely, I wasn't tired, not a bit. It must have been about 2 A.M. in the morning, or maybe a little later than that. That dawn breeze which had begun to lash our faces in the grassland was rushing through the car windows, hitting us, cooling and enervating. The car handled smoothly, emitting a deep humming noise clear against the backgrownd of the early dawn's eerie silence. We were now driving through the plains. There were a few scattered hills stuck in the plains like ancient monuments. There was one that looked as if some premordial giant had arranged a series of boulders into a pyramidal height. These hills at this hour of dawn assumed an ominous look. They stood silent, the only witnesses to our escape. Up till now, I was not sure where we were going. The northern road leads north, and my home is in the east.

Soon we crossed the river. The guard in the box was asleep. The river itself was asleep on its way to the ocean. My companion was still awake. We hadn't exchanged one word since we got into the car. He was now very withdrawn, distant, almost lost. Over him hung a vague sense of despair. I wanted to tell him all was all right, but he was not here in this old Peugeot driving towards the north.

We had now crossed the bridge and were driving into the country beyond the river. Then the idea hit me. Perhaps this was what I was doing all the time, without being aware. I was running home; I was taking my friend to the safest place I knew, to the village where I was born. Why did it not dawn on me before that this was what I was doing?

That thought gave me a new sense of life. I was both relieved and exhilirated. Relieved because for the first time that fateful night I knew where I was going. The flight from the bar, to the beach and the desperate dash through the grassland to the junction were all part of a design worked out by destiny. Exhilirated because now I knew where I was going. I was going home.

So I pressed on the accelerator. The old car leapt into the air, gaining speed. We were now passing by sleeping villages which lined the roads. Now and then two bright eyes of a wild cat would race into the forest. Along the route, I discerned the familiar cocoa trees, and the giant trees towering over the shorter trees shrouded in the gloom of the early dawn. Then we hit a deep mist in which I could hardly see anything in front of me. It looked as if my companion was asleep now. His breathing had changed from a regular smooth one to a jerky, now a throaty growl. The mist had come down from the mountain ranges now on our left. They are ranges I had always loved to watch, especially since I lived and worked in a small school on top of them years ago during a vacation. The hills were a solid black mass covered thick with mist this dawn.

The mist cleared when we descended the hills. We were speeding towards the grass country. We had to turn south now, leave the forest and swing right back. My companion was fully asleep, his head tossed behind him, his mouth slightly open. I noticed he had some iron fillings in his teeth. The dawn was breaking to our southeast. It was clearing out there, perhaps over the place where we were heading. It was coming slowly towards us. And we were moving fast towards that sunrise.

We were soon in the low orchard bush country, with the misty hills behind us. We passed through more sleeping villages. Cocks were crowing all over. Once or twice, I espied a farmer or a hunter on a path far across the distance by his lamp.

By the time we turned off the main road into the dirt track that led to my village, the dawn was clear. The sun was not yet up, but the skies were light. My companion was still asleep. In about half an hour I pulled up underneath the ancient tree outside our compound, I shook my friend awake. As we walked towards the homestead, I saw my uncle standing at the gate, his hands folded across his chest. As we came closer to him, he looked intensely in my eyes. He said, quietly. "Welcome, my son; I have been waiting for you."

I must have slept for hours, for when I woke up it was past noon. There was a bustle in the compound. My friend was still asleep on a mat in the corner. I stepped out of the room into the daylight. Women and children were everywhere. My uncle's wife, a tall jet black beautiful woman was leaning against the coconut tree. Immediately she saw me she rushed towards me. We embraced in silence because my uncle must have told her why I was home. Instinctively she understood that this was not the time for talking. A few relatives strayed into the compound. After the customary greetings, during which they asked about all my lovers, friends, masters, wives and every person with whom I had any contact in the great big city, they left us as leisurely as they came.

I was just about to step out of the compound then I met my uncle coming home from outside. He beckoned me to follow him. We went into his sacred room where he always took the most important visitors. This is the room that contains the paraphenalia of his diviner's art. He is a priest of Afa. He showed me a chair. He himself sat in his chair. He wore one of his wife's short cloths; his chest was bare. For what looked like a long indeterminate time, he stared silently into my eyes. I fidgeted for a while, but I soon calmed down under his gaze. Then he smiled.

"He is one of those people who left us long ago, isn't it?" he asked.

"What do you mean?" I asked.

"You don't know the story of those who left, taken away many years ago?" he asked.

"Yes, I know of it. I've read of them in books. But you mean my friend in there?"

"Yes," he said. "Yes, my father told me about them. His father told him."

He paused, his head intensely bent down upon the earth. An army of ants was on the march close by the wall.

"You see those ants there? You see how they walk in a file, their ranks closely kint? But anything can break their ordered march, smash the discipline and the progress of the march. And when that happens, there is chaos, confusion, destruction and death." His voice rose to a pitch. Then he paused, looking closely at me once more.

"But another time, one day, the ants will return to the rank, to the discipline of the tribe and the orderliness of the march. That becomes more important than the chaos and the disorder of earlier times."

"Yes, my father told me," he continued. "It was years and years ago, those were very dark days; night was upon the land. There was no rest. Men from the north, east, west and south came, even men who had eaten medicine with us. They were the companions of the whites who had been roaming our markets buying slaves. Then we heard there had been raids on the village of Chiemu. Children and women were rushing into our town screaming, some covered in blood. The slave raiders of the people north to this place were sweeping through the whole countryside. The men of our village took their guns and machetes, the warrior groups were ringed around the town. The war drums throbbing, the medicinemen stepped out into the sun, their fly whisks, talismans and sacred smocks weighing them down to their very knees. They cast the divining shells, but the owner of the earth had refused to tell them what lay in store. The death of a man hides behind his door. By late afternoon, the sun was flat and red against the sky. Silence was over the land. Then the raiders struck. Blood flowed. Many were captured. Some, including my great grandfather had fled into the bush. All his brothers had been captured and taken away. My father used to say to me, 'Do you know, your grandmother's children, and their offsprings took a boat to a land beyond the oceans? They are there.' But they say the snake that died on a tree will some day return to earth."

My uncle is normally a man of very few words. This had been one of his longest monologues. He stared outside into the coming sunset, his mind perhaps wandering away to some memories handed down to him by his father.

"Then there were those young men of the village of Menore on the coast who were deceived into going on board a European ship with their drums at the invitation of the captain. Their priests and divine leaders had warned them not to go. But they went. The European boat set sail with them and were soon lost between sea and sky. Till today, no one knows on which shores they landed."

I heard a stirring in the next room. My companion was up. He came to the door where we were. I opened it for him. He entered. My uncle showed him a low chair. He sat down. My uncle kept his eyes on the face of my companion who looked subdued and very quiet. None of the animation which enveloped him yesterday was present in his eyes. He had undergone a transformation the like I'd never seen before. My uncle looked at him for what seemed to be a long time. Then he suddenly shook his head and chuckled, a littly smile playing around his mouth.

"Didn't I tell you?," he said, turning to me now, "Didn't I tell you? Look at those hands. Look at those eyes. If he had been just a shade darker, I would have told you who he is. And if I meet him in a strange town I'll call his name, nay the name of his grandfather because he comes form our house. Look at his head, and the face. Look at him closely. Whom does he remind you of?" I was expected to answer this question. I raked my brain hard. Then I remembered. I remembered who this was. There was a distant cousin of mine who years ago dropped out of school because he simply could not cope with mental arithmetic. His name was Bawa. If he were alive now, and you saw him together with brother Lumumba, you would think they were twins who had slept in one womb. He had the face, the forehead, nose, especially the mouth of the people of Bawa's household. When I mentioned the name of Bawa, my uncle nodded approvingly.

A young shy girl, hardly seventeen or eighteen, entered the room after saying "agoo". She knelt down beside my uncle and whispered something in his ears. My uncle showed no sign of having heard what the girl said. Then she rose up and walked out. I knew most of my female relatives. But I had never set eyes on this one. I was struck by her beauty. She was very black; her skin was shiny. Her eyes were brightly lit, large, sleepy like a little lake beneath cool bushes tucked away from the disturbing feet of men and beasts. Her neck was covered with graceful folds, in rings. Her head was closely cropped. She wore a short upper garment which betrayed the profile of two strong throbbing breasts that stood like twin fruits on a beautiful tree. Her lower garment was a short cloth that came to her knees on which were two sets of blue beads. There were two rings of beads on her ankles. Her bare feet firmly gripped the earth as she walked. She brought into the room the beautiful smell of camwood and some other spices whose names in English I do not know. My companion was apparently woken up from his reverie by her entrance. He kept his eyes riveted on her face as she whispered to my uncle and kept them on her till she walked out.

"Who is she, my uncle?" I asked. He seemed to ignore the question by the way his eyes failed to register any reaction to it. Then as if from a long forgotten time, he spoke:

"She is your second cousin, the daughter of your elder mother who went away to the forest area years ago. Your elder mother her husband and her other children are still there. But she has to come home. She came home before the last sowing season." He paused. Then, as if he was not even aware of the awesome nature of what he said. "She came home because she is not well." I didn't or simply couldn't ask him what was her ailment. There are some questions which must not be asked.

"How long will you be staying with us?" my uncle asked. I answered that I was on leave from work and just decided to visit home. My uncle knew that I wasn't telling him our real reason for being home. But he understood. He turned his eyes upon my companion again, stared hard at him for awhile, smiled and shook his head again. Brother Lumumba smiled. My uncle extended his right hand to him, shook him firmly, snapped his fingers as we do, and said to him in our language, "My son, you are welcome." Then he rose up and left the room.

The evening was fast falling. The sun was hanging behind the tall ago palm tree on which weaver birds used to nest when I was a boy. Chicken, goats and other domestic animals were beginning to seek their sleeping places. Farmers were coming home from the distant farms.

After the evening meal(during which my friend started to eat with his left hand. I begged him to change to the right hand before my uncle came), I decided to take him through the village whose name I cannot call for diplomatic reasons. It is an old village. No one knows how old it is. You may come across a good number of its residents who will tell you a set of fantastic stories about its genesis. These include an ancestor who was a great magician. The village is built in a valley where they say spirits of those who died in war were still active. This illustrious founder of our village was said to have armed himself with all the magic of the land and went into the valley single-handed. He stayed in this valley in which he wanted to settle his people for seven days and seven nights. There he wrestled with the ghosts of the war dead, those who had died the death of blood and were supposed to be the most malevolent spirits of the hidden world. When he had been gone for four days, the other leading medicinemen, diviners, magicians, and priests who had camped at the edge of the forest waiting debated whether they should go down the valley and seek their leader. There was a great division. Some of them opposed the suggestion. But in the end, they were persuaded by one of the oldest men in the clan to desist from pursuing their spiritual leader. He told them that once he descended into that valley, he had actually been tranformed into a spirit force whose power was more terrible than a thousand ghosts. Anyone who dared to follow him will only have himself to blame for the horrible retribution that will be visited upon him by the combined power of all the invisible creatures of the valley. To cut a long story short, the old man's wisdom prevailed. And on the seventh night, at early dawn, the founder of the village returned, wet with dew, his feet muddy, his eyes ablaze, but his steps firm. That same day, he led my people into this valley where they built a prospering village by a river, on a wonderfully rich farming land.

We walked the narrow lanes guarded by the fading light throughout the seven sections distinguished by shrines and temples, meeting grounds and squares, and the little night markets lit by open lights from oil lamps. We met a few people on the lanes who insisted on knowing who my friend was. That's how my village people are, inquisitive, querying and down-right nosy if you let them. And if you didn't let them, your woes will be more terrible than if you simply said something very innocent like "Oh, he is my friend" to which they reply "Oh, I see. Stranger, welcome." I taught my friend to respond with a certain word which he enjoyed saying very much.

We heard drums coming from one section of the village whose children used to play with us. It was a lovers' drum. We went to the square. It was only a practice section because they were preparing for the moonlight season after the year's first harvest, six weeks away, so there wasn't much to see. We soon drifted back home. The night was deep upon us.

The drums were very close to our sleeping rooms. At first it was part of a dream, a weird galloping dream in which there were dancers, and a procession. But it was faint, far away. When I woke up in pursuit of the dream I was covered in sweat. My friend had apparently also been up, unable to sleep. He was sitting on his reed mat covered with white sheets.

He had folded the mosquito net because it was simply too hot to sleep underneath it. The drums were very close, rising on the waves, now faint far away, now throbbing right underneath the caves of our roof.

I looked at my wrist watch. The time was one in the morning. I stepped out into the *ablada,* and through it onto the compound. The direction of the drums was clear now. The music was coming from the eastern side of the village from the shadow of the ago palm. I knew that beneath that tree was the medicine hut. I used to be mortally scared to go near it as a boy because even though its custodian was one of my elder uncles, I was always afraid of his wild look, red eyes and brusque manners. Whenever he wanted to be pleasant to us the children he only always very nearly succeeded in frightening us. He served as the guardian of not only the medicine hut but also the ancestral shrine.

I went back indoors and motioned my companion to follow me. We stood on the compound for sometime. The sky was deep, dark, and ominous. The drums and human voices raised in song were the only sounds that broke the great silence of this dark night. I set out upon the way towards the drums. I knew my way to the shrine. I had grown up to lose all my fear of this shrine, that crippling terror of childhood which even infant curiosity could not once overthrow. It was long after I had left, gone to college and become an adult that anytime I passed by it, even though a faint shudder went through my whole body in remembrance of my youth, I would recover and look upon it only as an important landmark in my rather uninteresting life.

We plunged into the night, searching our way through the darkness to the drums. I could sense a vague fear that had overcome my companion. But somehow he felt safe that I was there.

We soon came to a small square lit by a dozen or so oil lamps. I halted. The drummers were facing where we were standing. We were shielded by the darkness. There were three drummers, and a small group of others playing rattles and gongs. In the circle a girl was dancing naked from the waist up. Her body glistened with sweat. There was a long bead around her neck hanging right down to the space between her two firm and erect breasts. Her dance was slow, marked by deliberate movement of feet, hands and her head, first to this side then to the other side. In the circle, moving around her with a fly whisk in his hand, was a man wearing a short smock. Then the lights from the oil lamps threw a beam on the faces of the two. The man was my uncle, the girl the young maiden who was said to be my cousin, the one said to be unwell. We retreated into the safety of the shadows in order to watch this ceremony.

I remembered a ceremony such as the one we were witnessing now when I was a child. I had gone with my mother to seek protection against witchcraft. I remembered the beginning of the ceremonies; my uncles, who officiated, looked different, distant. But a combination of fatigue and fright drove me into the arms of sleep. Big boy though I was (I must have been six) my mother put me on her back. Ever since, whenever I hear the medicine drums, my memory jumps back to that particular childhood night.

The drums picked up in tempo. There were about five or six singers, all women, whose voices sent up an eerie, sad, heart-rending song into the air to the background of the drums. The girl continued her dance which looked as if she was searching for something in the rising dust. My uncle, whose loose movements at first seemed like a stroll, was actually dancing an authoritatively gallant and assertively masculine dance. It was clear that he was the one in charge of this nocturnal ceremony. My grand uncle who was the custodian of the shrine was nowhere in sight.

The tempo of the drums increased. The girl began to strain in her search, to scatter her gestures. My uncle's dance became a fast walk, punctuated by quick deliberate strides. His eyes had assumed a fiery glare, his fly whisk whirling now as his hands and feet moved in fast dancing strides. Then suddenly, he paused. His feet astride, his head thrown back, his eyes scanning the dark night beyond the oil lamps. Then he moved his eyes in what looked like an aimless search in the skies; again he moved upon the drums, every step a dance step, a slow variation of the quick agile movement called forth by the drums which were throbbing across the deep night into our very stomachs. His eyes were still upon the dark skies, scanning the universe. The songsters' voices were clear, ringing across the night, sending out an eerie, sad, wailing funeral chant. Then as if from nowhere, the full moon appeared in the east, yellow, round. It came very very slowly as if on the wave of the golden orb that hung suspended in the vast empty darkness of the night sky. She was accompanied by a few stars which have now lined her route, as if they were sign posts. When my uncle saw her, he paused. His eyes scanned the heavens in a rolling gaze. He returned, borne back from the realm to which he had been transported, to the immediacy of the glowing lamps, the drums now in a quick celebrative mood, the drummers glistening in their sweat. He resumed his dance, now a dignified pacing assured step which showed he had returned.

The girl's dance, during the short period when the moon was coming, had become a mad twirling gyration. Her feet moved as if they were not touching earth. Her face was no longer distinguishable from the night as she swung in a circular movement around the drummers, around my uncle. The chant was shrill now. Then as if on a signal, she stopped. The drums continued to beat. She just stood where she stopped, her body drenched in sweat. She began to scan the darkness. She cleared the sweat from her eyes with her left hand. The drums had changed from a fast beat now to a slow funeral one. The singers too had changed their song. My uncle was now pacing the circle, a perplexed look on his face. The girl moved, first to the left then to the right. Then she moved backward, and as if impelled by an invisible force; she rushed forward, past those on the edge of the circle toward us, and as if held down, she stopped in her track, her eyes focusing the darkness where we were. Without warning, she burst into tears, accompanied by loud uncontrollable sobbing. The tears rushed down her face. She stood at the edge of the circle, her body convulsing in a fit of weeping. My uncle went close to her, placed his right hand upon her forehead. He took her by the arm and led her back towards the drummers, through them behind towards the blue curtain of the shrine. They were gone for almost a second when the girl burst into the circle again, as if pursued by an invisible demon. She leapt into the circle in a dance, twirling in a slow deliberate gait. The singers had changed their song into a soft moan led by the shrill voice of an anonymous singer. The moon now hung behind the circle, perched at the tip of the ago palm, suspended right above the shrine.

My uncle rushed out of the blue curtained shrine accompanied by a young boy carrying a herbal pot. The chant had changed again. The drums continued now muffled in a rumbling anger. There was a stormy look on his face. The girl stood on the edge now whimpering, staring into the darkness toward where we were. My uncle motioned the boy to put down the herbal pot. He tossed a fistful of alligator pepper into his mouth as he mumbled something to himself. He dipped the whisk into the pot, sprinkled the air towards the point of the rising sun, then to the place of the setting sun, then to the ocean, and finally to the forest and the desert lands. As if on cue, two men leapt out, caught hold of the girl and almost carried her to where my uncle was. She was slobbering saying something which I couldn't hear. The two men held her head as my uncle bathed her with the dripping water from the herbal pot.

It was at this point that my companion began to fidget, began to twiddle his fingers. We had not exchanged one word since I led him into the night. I could smell the special fragrance of *defetsyo,* the dominant herb in the medicinal cure which I had learned to pick since a boy. My companion began to sniff the air. Then he began to mumble something to himself. Then, as if on command, he stepped out of our hiding place into the domain of the night. Then he broke into a trot, and before I knew what was happening, he had burst the outer edge of the circle and was standing in the middle. There was a look of fascination, and an indescribable contentment upon his face. The girl, now drenched in herbal water that had just been used to wash her head was standing facing my companion. My uncle was moving toward the two of them, a flame of certainty now burning in his eyes, as if at last he had found the answer to a riddle. I've seen that look on his face after many sessions of his divination work. Then I heard my name echoing through the night. It was my uncle's voice. I stepped out of the dark, walked into the yellow light towards the edge, I saw my companion lying on the earth. Over him was bending the girl, now beaming smiling wildly and saying something about her husband having come home from the journey to the forest and desert land where he went to hunt. "You have come," she said, "returned home to the place I prepared for you. A man, a certain man, my husband, my elder, my hunter, the brave one. You promised to come with your companions. Welcome, welcome all of you, you are welcome" The two men were already carrying my friend into the shrine. My uncle put his hand on my shoulders and said,

"My son, everything is all right. Let us go." Then we walked back to the homestead. And the sun was rising far away in the yellow east. The moon had long since set.

After the noon meal, I sat on the compound staring into the skies. My aunts, uncles and other relatives walked through the compound, and after exchanging greetings with me, would walk away as if they did not know of what happened in the night. When the sun had mounted its horse, my uncle returned from a journey, a bundle under his armpit. We exchanged greetings. He put his hand upon my shoulders again, looked hard into my eyes, then walked into his sacred room. I soon heard his voice mumbling incantations that I had come to take for granted at any time I was home.

That day and the next were uneventful. I had still not seen my companion. On the third day, the rains came crashing through the trees accompanied by thunder, loud bangs, muskets fired through the forest and among the trees. The rain started before the dawn and continued till the late afternoon. I couldn't step out of the *ablada* where I sat in a wooden chair close to the door. I just stared at the rain falling upon the world. This was the third day since I saw my uncle. My aunt, my uncle's wife, when I asked her said he had gone to the town of Vanu which was towards the rising sun, about a day's walk. But uncle had ridden his old Raleigh bicycle. And he would return today but for this rain which might prevent him from setting out at dawn, the time he loved to travel. I ate my noon meal alone. It is no exaggeration to say that for these three days I was numb, as if I was on the verge of receiving some revelation whose very nature I felt I knew. I was still looking at the rain when the figure of my uncle crouched upon his aging bicycle rode into the homestead. He carried the cycle into the *ablada,* and then proceeded to peel off his wet jumper, his lower garment, a long short made of cloth from his own loom, and a white sleeveless singlet which he had worn wrongly (I knew because the manufacturer's label: "Made in England" was sticking outside). There was a buoyancy in his voice as he greeted me, and began to talk about the rain.

"That was quite a rain, my son," he said. "Rains like that don't fall anymore. It is the kind of rain in which sometimes the owner of the earth travels. Those who possess the eyes can see him walking in the rain, thunderbolts crashing around him, but as dry as you who hadn't stepped into the rain. That was the kind of rain in which your grandfather found the sacred axes upon which he built the shrine. But how have you been, my son?" I told him I was fine, but still tired. "Oh, you must drink some of your aunt's pepper wine. It is very soothing; besides it clears the fever form the blood. The fever has been running around these days. I have advised many to drink the pepper wine, but the fools think that I am drumming up trade for my wife." I wanted to tell him that the people were right. But I didn't. I was silent because there were other things on my mind. My uncle understood me, but he also knew and always said I was young; I had not even set out on the journey which he had designed for me.

The rain became mere trickles by early afternoon. The earth sent up that powerful after rain's musty and lusty smell of simple dust, trees and leaves, exhalations that spoke of a primeval time. The sun broke out soon, blazing now right over the ago palm tree and behind the shrine. My uncle, after hours in his sacred room, came into the *ablada,* a whiff of the sacred herbal ointment he always rubbed on his body around him. He pulled his cloth chair and sat down. And for about three hours, we both sat in complete silence. Slowly the sun moved westwards casting long shadows across the wet earth. I stepped out then to see my village, serene, calm after the rain, almost somnolent now in the falling sun. I watched the sun go down quickly, terminating that brief twilight of our clime.

I went back into the room. My uncle was still in his easy chair. He was smoking his short homemade pipe. I had never become used to the tobacco since childhood. I had a short grand aunt who had the annoying habit of puffing the smoke into our infant eyes. The tobacco was locally grown; every farmer kept a little patch on the edge of his corn or bean fields where this thin leaved tobacco was grown. They were cured by being hung on bamboo railings over the kitchen fire. At times they are treated in special herbal pomades made from shea-butter. The room was howling with the smell of this tobacco when I walked back. I sat down in my old place, my mind going over the events of the past days. I was still on this mental journey when I heard my name. It was my uncle. I responded as I should in the custom of my people. "Come with me, my son," he said. He was already standing up. It was early evening; darkness had already covered the world. Man, beast, spirit and man were indistinguishable.

Our way wound through the familiar lanes towards the eastern end of our division, towards the ago palm. I knew we were headed for the shrine. I had difficulty in finding my way, since we were on a different path. But I felt my uncle was far ahead of me somewhere penetrating the darkness with his sharp eyes. He was waiting for me on the dark empty square where I had witnessed the events of three nights ago. We walked together into the shrine through the blue curtain. There was an oil lamp burning low upon a low table in one corner. The room was empty. Its floor was made of earth. There was another room ahead whose door was shut. Sitting on a mat was a man with only a thin cloth around his waist. He was being fed from a clay bowl by a girl. They didn't even lift up their eyes when we walked in. I looked hard through the faint light. The man was my companion and friend, brother Lumumba. The girl was my cousin who was undergoing cure, she whose cure ceremony we witnessed three nights ago.

Brother Lumumba looked very relaxed, his eyes clear, and his countenance bathed in the glow of an inner light. The girl was also at peace. Her gestures were calm, almost fluid, as she returned the empty spoon from my friend's lips to the bowl to scoop up more of its contents. Her left hand was carefully placed upon his right leg bended in a sitting posture which I knew was the eating and divining posture of our shrine. My uncle motioned me to crouch in the corner beside the lamp where he himself was now crouched in the regular religious posture. The two people had still not shown any sign that they were aware of our presence.

The girl had finished feeding my friend. She rose up and walked slowly towards the table. She picked up a bowl of herbal pomade. She returned to him who was crouched on the mat. She sat down like our women do. Then she stretched her legs. She dipped her three middle fingers in her right hand into the coppery tin and began to rub the ointment on brother Lumumba's upper body. Her long thin delicate fingers moved deftly over his broad chest very hard. She looked into his face and said something to him. He turned round and lay face downwards exposing his broad brown back. She began from around the lower part of his back to his waist. She was kneeling beside him now. A small bead of sweat was on her forehead, just above her dark bright eyes. She began now, deliberate, slow, working up a rhythm, soft, sibilant, touching. Brother Lumumba's body was heaving up and down syncopating, alternating with the girls' movements. She moved gently up his back till his neck, where she lingered for awhile. When she finished, my friend rose up, turned round and sat on the mat. The girl went to the long water pot in the opposite corner. She dipped her hand in the pot and brought up a calabash full of water. The calabash must have been left in the pot. She gave the water to him. He received it with both hands. Then he threw back his head and began to drink, his Adam's apple racing up and down. When he finished, he handed the calabash back to her. There was a smile on his face. The contentment I saw when we returned had now become an unfathomable radiance. She stood the calabash over an empty bowl. She returned to the mat where he was now sitting, his left leg bent, the sole of his feet firmly resting on the mat, his right leg folded underneath him. She sat down, her legs stretched out, smiling. They sat like that for a long time without saying a word. After a long time she started a song. I knew it as a child. I can only give you a free translation:

> The winds from the rivers blow here,
> The rivers flow into the body of the land,
> Night, day, light, dark;
> Trees and rivers, cousins or air
> Will fall into the pot.

You see, this was a children's song, which we knew was full of nonsense words. You sang it as a child, but forgot it as soon as you grew pubic hairs. But she had taught this song to my friend, and soon he too joined in singing the words as if he had been familiar with them all his life. They sang it twice over. Then she said to him it was time to sleep. She rose up and out of a box removed the mosquito net. She tied the strings on pegs on the four corners on the walls. He lay down his head on the pillow. She brought a big cover cloth from the box and covered him. She greeted him with the night greeting. She threw the mosquito net over him. She picked up the oil lamp, opened the door behind the mat. She went in and closed the door.

Uncle and I were left in the dark. I felt his arm on mine as he steered me out. And the night enveloped us as we walked through the alleys on our way home.

The winds from the rivers blow here, the rivers flow into the body of the land; night, day, light, dark; trees and rivers cousins of air will fall into the pot.

ON THE DAWN OF THE FIFTH DAY after the lull and the calm of the inconsolable sea, the skies burst open in a fury of thunder and storm. Our craft which once had looked formidably large even in the face of the ocean was borne on the waves of the howling winds, whipped and lashed in an unwarned fury that raged for days. In our holds, already reduced in spirit and flesh by the agony of our fate, on this lachrymose graveyard afloat, we were ready to step cold-blooded into this new torment which could yet be our salvation. We hear the song, prohibitive, its voice slashed and barbed, wounded beyond time. All over, in the vortex of the darkness, were the bodies of our companions paralyzed by the total mystery of our fate. The craft rose and fell, caught in the spasm of dying in the throes of the beginning, crashing and crushing us as we lay in our captive chains. For days we lay in our vomits, in the pungent smell of the sick and the dying in that overwhelming scent of our ultimate humanity.

The storm abated on the tenth day. It abandoned us as suddenly as it came. We lay spent and weary. It looked as if the once defeated sun had appeared, invisible to us in our prison, but emitting even into the dungeon its light and benevolence, restoring for us a brightening hope. On that first day of calm, some of our captors who themselves must have been sick, appeared to check our numbers and to reassure themselves of the safety of their goods. The dead were removed. They returned to the upper world abandoning us the survivors once again to our calamitous dreams.

Day after day in the lethargy of this calmness, the voyager was coming, brought along by more than chance, the ocean, its peopled seas, and the inviolable sun. Soon, soon, he would be home.

I WOKE UP WHEN WE SWUNG into the valley. My memory could not focus the events of the past forty-eight hours. My mind had been a maze of sensations ever since I landed here. Where was I now? Where were we heading? I remember the man driving the car vaguely. Soon, he looked at me and smiled. I returned his smile, but I could not grasp the meaning of it all.

The valley extended before our eyes, vast into the coconut groves on the far shore of what looked like a lake in the distant horizon. The morning air was brisk and cool. My sleep had been fitful. I tried hard to return to the most recent events beyond the exhiliration of my journey to Africa but all was blurred by time and memory.

We were soon riding on a dirt road, past quiet villages. We drove into a village just when the full dawn had burst upon us. An old man in a small loin cloth received us at the entrance of a large compound fenced with living trees. He and my companion exchanged some words in their language. We were shown a room which was dark, the silhouette of carvings against the wall on a low table. Our beds were reed mats with single pillows. I lay me down and slept the longest sleep of my entire life.

I was home. A little boy, slightly older than in the last dream time. It was twilight, with the glowing setting sun suspended over the hills beyong the valley. A few lights were on in the dim hill-top houses. My mother's voice was coming out of the living room distinctly humming a hymn, one of those many favorites of hers in the changing seasons of her Christian piety. None of my brothers and sisters were home. Father too wasn't home. Something heavy was pressing on my heart as I sat facing this twilight all by myself. Not even my mother's voice was part of my world now. It was as if it came from an unknown region, haunting yet sweet, bearing the burden of its own distinct sorrow. I was sitting still, my eyes riveted upon the valley and the hills beyond.

Then I heard the jangle of the chains, coming from the east towards the lower hills above the valley. A monody that I have heard before clear now also rose above all other sounds. It was again my mother's voice, this time raised in a chant above the hills. Fear gripped me instantly. I rose up. And as suddenly as my eyes focused the road before our house and the valley, they beheld a long line of men, women and children linked by a trailing chain. Their footfalls made a rhythmic thud upon the hurting earth. The monody was above them in the hills. To its harmonic cadence the falling feet provided the beat. I beheld them as if for eternity, fascinated and afraid. Then the procession underwent a transformation before my eyes. It was now the familiar funeral cortege without the body, the funeral cele-brants in black robes, the children in front, women in the middle, and the men bringing up the rear. Suddenly I began to recognize the faces of the people. I saw my father on the far edge towards the fields, slightly stooped, his hat in his hand. Then my brothers and sisters scattered among the mourners, intensely staring in my direction. At the rear of the women was my mother, apart, alone, her mouth closed but her solitary deep rich voice providing the dirge to which the procession wound its way towards where I knew not. Panic seized me. They were leaving me behind. They were going away somewhere and no one cared to invite me to come along. I was being deserted in this valley while my people, my flesh and blood, were walking away in the company of strangers. Tears welled up in my eyes. I raised up my voice and shouted. But no one heard me. My brothers and sisters had turned their faces away now towards the west, towards the departing sun. I had flung my hands into the air. I raced down the valley, threw myself into a quick fall that was broken by the lonely maple on the edge, but I did not reach them; they passed before me, the fall of their feet more distinct now than ever, the single voice of their accompanying hymn, clearer than a thousand organs. I could not reach them.

Then slowly, I turned my face away, their footfalls and the music behind my back. I traced my steps from the edge of the valley, from the maple, the hills at my back, towards our porch. When I arrived at the foot of the short stairway, I was weary, tired, as if I have been stretched over a rack, whacked by a thousand blows. I turned round. The procession had gone. But now, as distinct as before, I heard the music of the jangling chains and the monody still in the valley. As clearly as I could, I heard it; the footfalls continued in their thumping rhythmic beat upon the earth: But the prisoners, and the mourners were gone.

I sat upon the porch and in my dream, wept. When I woke up, it was night, as it was in the beginning.

After the evening meal, my companion and I wandered the village awhile. When we came back, the old man was sitting in his low khaki-cloth armchair. He motioned us to the seats opposite him. For over something like an hour, he and my friend spoke in their language. I knew they were talking about me because their eyes, especially those of the old man, were upon me. Now he would let off a chuckle, shake his head and deliver a smile that was the most benign I'd ever seen. It looked as if the old man was telling my companion some story to which the latter was paying intense attention. I listened, not understanding a word, but drinking in the music of their voices, somewhere recalling from the deep recesses of my being the deep resonance of this strange tongue which could have been once upon a time my own.

The night was silent outside but for the crying of insects

and the hooting of an owl on a nearby tree. The silence was soothing against the background of the old man's voice which now was a deep rumbling river gurgling through some deep primeval forest, now soft like the murmuring thunder of the early night rain. Sometimes, it was only a cooing whisper that caressed the vague light of the little lamp behind which I could behold the bright eyes of my companion locked in an animated attention which I had never felt before. The old man would now and then let off a quiet laughter which was more in retrievance of some event down the alley of his memory than in joy or ecstasy. It yet bespoke of a hidden pain, recognizably deep beyond time itself, a pain that sought to include me in its orbit, uneasily reminding me of my own. But it was a shared pain, without the relentless emphasis of the absence of joy, love, or compassion.

After what looked like eternity, the old man gave me his right hand. I shook it, and we snapped our fingers the way I have come to recognize the companionship of greeting that underlies all linking bonds. Then he left us to go to his room.

I could not have been asleep for more than an hour when I was woken up by a start. The music of drums and a chorus of voices were right beneath the flimsy walls of where we slept. Then the music was far away, now faint, yet clear. I noticed my friend was also sitting up. I had never heard this kind of music before. There was something eerie, weird about it, especially the shrill female voices of the chorus that seemed to be suspended on the air waves long after the drums had ceased to be a voluble echo of the deep and fearful night. I sat on my mat and for the first time since my sojourn here, I was afraid. The same panic that seized me in my dream of loneliness had taken hold of me. No. I was not afraid for my life, I was apprehensive of the powers of this dark night, powers that the voices and the drums seemed to be releasing into the world, or which, without recollection and memory, I knew were part of my torment yet.

My companion rose up from his mat. He quickly put on his clothes. He motioned me to do the same. When I was ready, he beckoned me to follow him.

I stumbled after him into the deep night through what was a maze of narrow lanes between the walls. Our way wound as if in a circle as we searched the night for the place of the music. Now, we heard the drums behind us, now in front of us, now very close by, now in the vague distance of what could have been a thousand miles away. At one point, I could not see my companion. I stretched out my hands into the darkness before me. I touched him. He gripped my hand to keep me from falling. Then, like a blind man, I was led through the deepening tunnels of the village night into the depths beyond, towards the passion of the drums.

We came to a small clearing dimly lit by oil lamps. My campanion halted. In front of us was a small group of drummers and dancers, surrounded by a little circle of people. This was where the music came from. The drums were sending a brisk rhythm into the air, behind the cluster of women and men was the chorus. There was a girl in the center, shuffling her feet in quick sturdy steps, searching the rising dust beneath her feet with her scanning eyes. In the circle with her was an elderly man in a dark smock covered with what looked like square pouches of leather. He was circling the girl in what at first seemed a casual unstudied walk, but on closer look was in fact a dance, a gentle gaited dance of feet and hands, elegant, with lifted head and raised torso, his countenance sending a penetrating search into the sky.

It took a while for my eyes to become used to the darkness. Then the profiles and the faces began to clear. The dancing maiden was the strikingly beautiful girl who came to the room the previous evening and spoke to the old man. When she walked in, I knew I had seen her before, but I could not remember where. I wanted to ask my companion who she was, but there was simply no time or occasion. The man who was dance-walking around her was the old man, my companion's uncle.

The drums soon changed their beat from an agile and brisk to a slow and deliberate one. The dancing girl had also moved into a more self-conscious step. The old man had paused, his gaze fixed upon the heavens, upon the silhouette of the tall palm tree. After a brief moment, the moon, a large golden orb appeared as if summoned. A chorus of singing voices greeted it, the drums beat a quick rolling salutation. As if upon a signal, the rhythm changed again. The girl's dance became wilder. She was now actually on the run, seeking to burst out of the circle. Then she paused suddenly staring into the night at where we were covered by the darkness, tears streaming down her head now on the lap of the old man. Slowly he began to bathe her face with water from a pot placed before him. The drums were now playing singular beats like a march without intervals. The voices were silent. The moon hung overhead, red and ominous.

THE LANDSCAPE WAS THAT ONE I KNEW in the primeval clarity of the absence of time, the sacred moments of pain and joy, in the combined miracle of birth and death, in the only reality of my body fate and destiny. It was a sweeping valley, verdant, clotted here and there by the tallest trees of creation. The birds, led by the Bird, were a flock of dazzling arcs and colors circling the tallest trees. Underneath, upon the earth, the Man was finishing the last offering, preparing the offals for the altar on the lowest hill beneath the Tree. It is this that the birds were hovering over, awaitng it seemed, their summons to partake of the sacrifice. They carried the Woman, laid her on the earth, her face shining with a power that was indescribable. Her beads were loose on her body. She was limp. Her eyes were glazed. She was borne by two tall men in loin clothes. The Moon, fiercly red, was suspended. Through the valley beneath the altar mountain flowed the river, the sister of the ocean whose rumble I heard beyond the hills. From here, I received the intimate knowledge of the mosaic structure of my first contact with infininity. So the invulnerable arena of my soul was part of the landscape, of the magical leaping feat of the Fish, the purest witness to my premordial pain. I myself took on the wings of the Bird, the fins of the Fish, the towering height of the Tree, the eternity of the River and the depth of the Ocean. I was the Man, the Woman, and the Child on the voyage between earth and sky, in the thrill of the perilous flight of all things. But my solitude was adamant, as I hung between life and earth, death and sky, treading my assumptions and distinct disabilities underfoot. I was the invincible essence of the rising phoenix, of the undying animal of all our humanity. Here the dead lily of the vanquished desert was blooming again; alive again were the creepers and lichens of the inconsolable forest, the flying corridors of heaven, the brown elephant grass of the savanna, the nurturing home of the elemental seed. This conglomerate, this ultimate was spelt by the vision of the girl among the scents, the excitation of the birds, the joy of the fishes and the ecstasy of the wild lilies. The suspended and preoccupied moon, destitute passion of my rebirth, was the cleansing force washing away the hate and calamity I once bore.

I alighted now at the last edge of the valley. The music that had once become a slow monotone had changed into a clanging celebrative din of drums, cymbals, bass guitars, trombones, and the quivering voice of shivering trumpets. Then, as if in response to the music's call, the whole valley burst into life. There poured into it from nowhere a host of men, women, children, and flocks of birds that darkened the face of the moon, trailed by stars across the heavens shooting at quick intervals into the valley. The people were of all the colours of the earth, pale, pink, red, brown, black, Europeans, Jews, Asians, Africans, each group in its colorful clothes. Among them were some with heads reaching to the skies, some whose feet were turned inside out, some were dwarfs whose nearness to the earth hardly afforded them somersaulting room. Some were musicians playing all the instruments of the earth in a cacophonous din making the type of music the poet called the tumult of a mighty harmony that could frighten the deaf. There were drummers, flutists, oboists, guitarists, xylophonists, trumpeters. Then followed an army of magicians, jugglers, acrobats and sorcerers in whose hands all things were given birth and death, men who held the sky and the earth in lingering parley, released with their mouth the hidden essence of all things, restoring the unity of ALL by the power of the WORD. And then came the gods and kings, the secret guardians of the Universe whose brothers were the Bird, the Tree, the Mountain, the River and the Ocean. They flew like the wind on galloping horses across the valley, cried like the howling thunder, destroyer and unifier. At the last tip came the infants accompanied by the wild beasts the lion, the leopard, the tiger, the wolf, the hyena, led by the smallest child on their way to the festival.

Then I heard my name called thrice in the mouth of thundering cannons, poignant. I stepped out behind the procession towards the mountain altar. But my walk was a flight. I was being borne to where the woman lay. Through the hosts, through the animals whose smells I bore in my nostrils, through the midst of the musicians and their deafening sounds, through the vortex of the purifying fire I emerged, swooping now, settling over the universe, resting by the side of my love. Then the children came forward and touched me, caressed me with their infant hands. They were of all colors as the men and women. They breathed upon me their infant breaths exuding the primal scent of sweet barks out in the winter. Then the animals came to where we lay, nuzzling and rubbing their snouts against my face and forehead. Then the gods and the king, the meekest of them all, benevolence emanating from their countenances. After this interminable libation in which I was bathed in tears, sweat, saliva and the passionate incenses from the mouths of the sorcerers, the children and the gods, we were left alone on the mountain, she and I. The old man was bending over us; his breath sweet, his eyes the brown colour of the earth. She to whom I was summoned was sitting upon the reed mat on the altar. Her hands were rested upon my brow. The old man spoke, now, he chanted a prayer. The valley was aglow with a bright incandescent light. The lingering mourning hymn had gone. The music was ended. Then I saw him retreating over the tallest hill, going. She and I were alone.

And I knew it was more than that, it was infinitely more than that.

Kofi Nyidevu Awoonor was born in the Asiyo division of Wheta in eastern Ghana. He was educated in the Catholic and Presbyterian Primary Schools of Dzodze and Keta, and later at the Zion College, Anloga and Achimota School. He holds degrees from the Universities of Ghana and London, and the State University of New York. He was professor in English and Comparative Literature in SUNY at Stony Brook, and professor of Literature at the University of Cape Coast, Ghana. He is presently Ghana's Ambassador to the UN. He has published several volumes of poetry, a novel, and a major book of essays on the history, culture and literature of sub-saharan Africa.

Comes the Voyager at Last is a tale told in poetry and prose. It is a haunting tale of slavery, the forced journey of the African to the New World and his subsequent return to the native land. Like Awoonor's first novel, *This Earth my Brother, Comes the Voyager at Last* is a work of mythic consciousness, an affirmation of the life forces of love and humanity in the face of the devasting forces of destruction characterized here in the historical racism that oppressed and continues to oppress black people both on the continent and in the diaspora. The mythic journey of the protagonist ends on the African soil, in a final act of reconciliation and atonement, in the miracle of love, in the affirmation of the black man's ultimate and enduring humanity.